W9-BAJ-156

AN AVALON ROMANCE

THE WRITE MATCH
Margaret Carroll

Kit McCabe may be a newly minted associate editor at New York's most exclusive bridal magazine, but her personal life owes more to bad karma than to romance. That is until she falls into a cab with Wall Street player Mark Dawson III, who is gorgeous, funny . . . and engaged to be married.

Mark Dawson's work may be risky business, but his loyalty to friends and family runs deep. He knows the wedding is a mistake, but it would be damaging to his fiancée and her career to call it off now. To make matters worse, Kit is covering their nuptials for her magazine and he can't seem to take his eyes off the lovely editor.

With the big day less than two weeks away, Kit and Mark struggle to hide their growing attraction to each other from everyone, including themselves.

THE WRITE MATCH

●

Margaret Carroll

AVALON BOOKS
NEW YORK

Published by Thomas Bouregy & Co., Inc.
160 Madison Avenue, New York, NY 10016

Library of Congress Cataloging-in-Publication Data

Carroll, Margaret, 1960–
The write match / Margaret Carroll.
p. cm.
ISBN 0-8034-9774-1 (acid-free paper)
1. Women periodical editors—New York (State)—New York—
Fiction. 2. Marriage service—Fiction. 3. Weddings—Fiction.
I. Title.

PS3603.A774587W75 2006
372.48—dc22
2005035232

PRINTED IN THE UNITED STATES OF AMERICA
ON ACID-FREE PAPER
BY HADDON CRAFTSMEN, BLOOMSBURG, PENNSYLVANIA

For Kathleen (my inspiration),
Rand (in loving memory), Mom, everyone at J-Spa
(especially Johnny for keeping the volume low)
and Tim O'Donnell.

Chapter One

Weddings, the Van Winterden Way: When greeting the groom, congratulate him on his good fortune.

Kit McCabe sprinted onto First Avenue in a heavy downpour, unaware that the next moment would change her life forever. Karma is like that.

Yanking open the door of a yellow taxicab, she practically fell into the arms of a stranger. "This one's mine," Kit said in her best I'm-practically-a-native-so-don't-even-try-it voice.

Then she got a look at the handsome man in front of her. Tall. Thick brown hair. Warm brown eyes. And a smile so perfect, he could be in a commercial for whitening strips. On second thought, she'd share the cab.

A bus roared by, spraying her from head to toe with New York City street water. Kit tried to duck, but lost her footing instead, and sprawled forward into the back seat of the cab.

1

The hunky stranger scooped her up, saving her. Kit felt two strong arms wrap around her, and decided it was a feeling she could grow accustomed to. She breathed in and got a whiff of Ralph Lauren aftershave mixed with something else—him. Nice. She looked up directly into twinkling eyes.

The handsome stranger grinned.

Kit completely forgot she was soaked to the skin and nearly frozen. "We can share the cab," she offered politely as though she were not already practically in his lap.

"Thanks." He looked as if he had just won the lottery.

Kit decided he must be from out of town, which rendered him "geographically undesirable." Too bad. At least she had the cab.

"Driver, two stops," he said. "The first is . . . ," he motioned to Kit with one hand.

"The Plaza."

The cab lurched away from the curb.

"Everybody should get to say that at least once," he said.

Cute. Kit shot him a quick, appraising glance. His features were refined, intelligent. She was glad she had not taken the bus. She reached up with one hand and smoothed her hair. It was always wild on a rainy day— the redhead's curse. So far, it had remained tucked into the ballet bun high on her head.

"I'm headed there, too, so you can make that just one stop," he said to the driver. "The Plaza." He smiled at Kit. "Now I got to say it, too."

He was funny. Kit smiled back, very glad she had taken extra care with her makeup that morning. She was headed to the single most important business meeting of her career—which reminded her she was running late. Kit checked her watch, only to discover she was not wearing one. She had forgotten it. She sighed, glancing up.

He looked away, out the window. He'd been watching her.

"Do you have the time?"

"Almost ten past," he said.

"Uh-oh," Kit groaned.

"Don't worry. You'll wow 'em. Blame it on the rain. That's what I'm going to do."

"Good plan." He had the sort of face that would look at home on the big screen, which mercifully took some of the sting out of the fact that she was now officially late. She found she couldn't take her eyes off him.

He ducked his head like a small boy, and Kit realized he was shy. He looked back at her, still smiling, then frowned. "Um, you've got something there." He pointed to a place high on her cheek. "A smudge."

Kit felt her cheeks turn hot—another redhead curse. "I do?"

"Here, let me," he said, reaching into his jacket pocket. He offered her a crisp white linen handkerchief with the letter *D* embroidered on one corner in navy blue.

He studied the rain-soaked streets outside while Kit dabbed her cheek.

"Did I get it?"

He turned to her and frowned, "Not quite."

Kit rubbed her hot cheek harder.

He shook his head, "Let me." Taking the handkerchief from her, he leaned in close and dabbed at something just below her right eye. His touch was gentle, despite his large hands. "Got it."

Kit was suddenly aware of the feel of her damp silk blouse against her skin and of the way her spring trench coat, now soaked through, clung to her curves. With him so near, she could see his brown eyes were flecked with gold. Definitely twinkling. His jaw was chiseled, with a dimple in the center. And he had a smile as bright as blue skies on an endless prairie. Kit let out a sigh of pure happiness.

He pressed the handkerchief into her hand. "Keep it. You never know when you might need it."

Chivalry was alive and well in Gotham.

Suddenly a flicker of tension crossed his face, as if he had just remembered he had left the tub running. His jaw tightened, he ducked his head again and moved back to his side of the cab. He checked his watch again, and took a swipe at his hair with one well-muscled hand—not that his hair needed smoothing. "Remember, blame it on the rain," Kit said with a smile. She had known him for just a few minutes, and already she hated to see him tense.

He smiled. "I'm meeting people in The Palm Court."

"Me, too." The Palm Court was the lobby restaurant of The Plaza Hotel, a favorite place for brunch among New Yorkers and tourists alike. It was not unusual that he would be headed there. Still, Kit had a sneaking suspicion, which put a damper on the small flame in her solar plexus.

He frowned. "Party of four?"

Kit nodded.

His eyebrows raised. "*White Weddings* magazine?"

She nodded. She could practically hear the hissing sound as the flame was doused.

"I'm Mark Dawson," he said, extending his hand.

Kit placed her hand in his. It was as warm and big and strong as it had seemed a minute ago. Which just made things worse, considering who he was.

"That makes you either Ethel Van Winterden, the famous wedding planner, or . . ."

"Kit McCabe, the not-so-famous associate editor of *White Weddings*," she said with a tight smile.

"That's funny," he said. "We're on our way to the same meeting, and wind up in the same cab."

At the moment, Kit did not feel like laughing. He was the most attractive man she had ever met, and he was officially off-limits. Spoken for. Taken. If she were another sort of woman, she would have pouted. Instead she gave him a small smile and nodded, "Karma."

"I beg your pardon?"

"Karma," Kit said again. It was a favorite expression her mother used to explain the seemingly random happenings in the universe. Karma meant that there were no coincidences in life, but only small lessons to be learned from each event as the universe revealed to each person his or her unique purpose in life—according to Kit's mother, anyway.

Mark gave a solemn nod.

He was from the Midwest, Grosse Pointe, Michigan, to be exact, as noted in the bio she had received from her editor. *Mark Dawson III. Up-and-coming financial analyst at MuniMoney, a blue-chip firm on Wall Street. Lake Forest graduate. Avid kayaker.* In short, the sort of man who fit Kit's profile of the perfect date—except for the fact that he had just won a free wedding, courtesy of the magazine Kit worked for. Her job was to write about his wedding, a prospect she was now looking forward to with all the enthusiasm she might muster for a root canal. "Congratulations," Kit said.

"Thanks. I had guessed you weren't Mrs. Van Winterden—unless you'd discovered the fountain of youth since they took the photo for the press kit."

Kit smothered a laugh at the reference to her major-domo boss, Mrs. Ethel Van Winterden, founding editor of *White Weddings* magazine, world-class authority on party etiquette, wedding planner to the stars, and author of a new coffee table tome, *Weddings, the Van Winterden Way.* Anxious brides could scour its thousand-plus pages for practical advice such as where to find rare orchids out of season or a full history on the timeless art of calligraphy. A bonus CD-*Rom* contained his and her to-do lists. Mark, however, didn't need the book. He had won a free wedding, courtesy of the publisher.

"Mrs. Van Winterden is a treasure," Kit said evenly. "You'll enjoy working with her."

"I'm sure I will."

He ran his hand through his hair again, watching the rain.

He looked as if he needed convincing. "This was all Ruby's idea," he said.

Ruby. It was a good name for a roller derby queen and obviously the nickname for Rachel Lucinda Lattingly, winner of a splendid wedding that would be planned to perfection by Mrs. Ethel Van Winterden herself. Winner of the *White Weddings* essay contest. Aspiring model. Sarah Lawrence grad. And soon-to-be Mrs. Mark Dawson III. Kit suddenly felt as if there was a pile of heavy, wet leaves in her stomach. She gave a small nod, all business now. "Trust me. Your wedding will be the talk of the town."

Mark glanced at her and their eyes locked. Something passed between them. It was a thought or perhaps a feeling. Kit couldn't be sure. Later, she'd chalk it up to karma.

The cab lurched to a stop across from the European-style piazza, complete with fountain and horse-drawn carriages, that made this section of Fifth Avenue so charming. Kit and Mark opened the door onto a red carpet. They had arrived.

"I've got this," Kit said, in a business-like tone as she dug through her Kate Spade bag in search of her wallet. Mark, however, had already taken control of the situation. He paid the driver, climbed out onto the sidewalk, and reached back into the cab for Kit. He pulled her out in one smooth motion, as if she weighed nothing at all.

The doorman sheltered them with an oversized umbrella while Kit got her footing on the red carpet.

Mark watched her. "Ready?" He placed his hand lightly and gently on her elbow, guiding her up the steps and into the lobby of the world-famous Plaza Hotel.

Kit was aware of him beside her, tall but not overly so. He had a powerful build. Rachel Lucinda Lattingly was a lucky girl indeed.

The strains of a violin greeted them as they made their way to the row of potted palms that gave the restaurant its name.

Mark smiled. "Oh, good. I can't eat unless there's a

string quartet." He was wearing his poker face. But his eyes gave him away. Definitely twinkling.

Kit sighed. This was going to be tougher than she wanted to admit. Her first cover story would be about the wedding of a man she wished she could have for herself. The realization jolted her like the sudden sweet taste of forbidden fruit.

Mark saw her flinch, leaned forward and asked, "You okay?"

"Fine."

"I'll wait here if you'd like to visit the ladies' first." He phrased it like a question, then added quickly, "But you look fine. I mean, wonderful." He looked her up and down, then caught himself and glanced away.

Kit shook her head. "Thanks." A trip to the Ladies' room was out of the question. She was already more than ten minutes late, in violation of one of Mrs. Van Winterden's basic rules of etiquette. Instead, Kit snuck a quick peek in a giant, gilt-framed mirror. Her blouse clung in places where her skin was still soaked, but the gold and black silk brought out the warm tones of Kit's complexion. Overall, it would do. Kit put on her best face, took a deep breath, and followed the maitre d' to the table.

Mrs. Van Winterden and Rachel Lucinda Lattingly would have been easy to spot even without help. They were seated at a choice table facing the entrance. Ethel Van Winterden was tiny but regal in a smart blue suit of boiled wool, complete with brass buttons. She wore one of her signature hats, a cloud-colored fedora with a small spray of forget-me-nots tucked onto the small brim. An homage to spring.

The woman perched at her side was tall—very tall—and heartbreakingly thin. Dressed head to toe in black, her ultra-straight, ultra-blond hair pulled into a tight ponytail, she leaned on one elbow, listening with rapt attention to Mrs. Van Winterden.

Kit walked through the dining room, her head held high as she readied herself to meet the founder of the magazine for which she was so proud to work. Mrs. Van Winterden was a woman whose photo often appeared in the society pages of *The New York Times*—Someone with whom Kit had once shared an elevator but hadn't dared speak to.

"You'll wow her," Mark whispered behind Kit. "Don't worry!" He gave her shoulder a quick squeeze which both surprised and encouraged her.

"Darling, hello. You're late," Ruby said by way of greeting. The tiniest suggestion of a frown flitted across her smooth forehead, beneath perfectly arched eyebrows. Ruby's complexion gave new meaning to the word *alabaster*, and made Kit wish she'd heeded all the warnings never to go outside without a heavy layer of sunblock.

Mark bowed and kissed his intended bride's cheek. Ruby wrapped one thin, bejeweled arm around his neck.

There were several thousand dollars' worth of David Yurman bracelets on that slender, pale wrist. The bracelets would need to come off for the big day, Kit noted.

"And who is this? Someone you rescued from the rain?" Ruby glanced, giggling, at Mrs. Van Winterden to see if she got the joke. "He's all heart." She turned her frosty blue gaze full on Kit. "Poor thing, you're soaked."

"Sweet pea, meet Kit McCabe," Mark said. "Kit, this is my bride-to-be, Rachel Lucinda Lattingly. You can call her Ruby for short."

Kit shook Ruby's hand, careful to avoid her long red nails. "I wish you all the best with the wedding, and your marriage." *Too bad I didn't meet him first,* she thought. "It is a pleasure to see you," she said, turning to Mrs. Van Winterden. *Manners,* Kit thought. *Don't act like you're meeting her for the first time. That would reveal the fact she hasn't spoken to you even once in almost three years.*

Mrs. Van Winterden extended a dainty, manicured hand in Kit's direction.

Kit shook it gently, as though it was made of Dresden china. "Have you met Mark Dawson?"

"My fianceé," Ruby piped as if they didn't know.

Mark grabbed Mrs. Van Winterden's doll-sized hand and pumped away. Too hard. Kit winced and realized he must be nervous, too.

"Congratulations, young man." Mrs. Van Winterden's voice was surprisingly strong, coming as it did out of her tiny, size-two frame. She was getting on in years, but appeared to have availed herself of every cosmetic procedure that existed to smooth the way. "I wish you both every happiness in the world," she added, in perfect observance of one of her own rules of wedding etiquette.

"Thank you," Mark replied. "I can't believe we won a free wedding. Makes a great story to tell the grandkids." He gave his bride-to-be a squeeze.

Ruby pulled away and quickly ran a hand across her head to make sure her hair had not been mussed.

She was obviously not the touchy-feely type, Kit thought.

Ruby's cell phone trilled the theme from *Sex and the City*.

Mrs. Van Winterden's delicate face rearranged itself as though she had just swallowed a bite of foie gras that was past its prime. Ruby apparently had not yet read the chapter on "Etiquette in Public Places." If she had, she would know that cell phones were taboo in five-star hotels and private clubs.

Ruby silenced the phone, stowing it away in her oversized Burka bag. "So," she turned to Kit, "you're the reporter who is going to tell the world all the news about our wonderful romance."

Kit bristled. "Reporter" was a title reserved for junior staff at regional newspapers, not editors at glossy national magazines. Kit had just been promoted to associate editor, a title that carried a certain amount of prestige—at least among Kit's fellow cubicle-dwellers.

"Hmm, yes," Kit said finally.

Mrs. Van Winterden studied Kit through the thick lenses of her signature half-frame tortoise-shell glasses. Her gaze never wavered.

Kit was grateful she had dressed with care, brushing her gold suede sling-backs before slipping them on over a new pair of sheer silk stockings. The shoes were now soaked through, splotched with gray, and ruined. Her black pencil skirt hung in limp wet folds around her knees. It was dry clean only. But rain made flowers grow. Another quote from Mom. Kit stood her ground.

A Palm Court waiter swooped in, pulling two chairs

out from the table with a flourish. He pushed Mark's chair in so close to Kit that their knees were touching.

Mark's leg threw off heat and Kit felt it spread along her thigh. In another minute, she was sure steam would rise.

The Maitre d' beamed. "Now that the happy couple has been seated, I will serve you a wonderful brunch."

Kit felt her cheeks flush. She and Mark were not the "Happy Couple." Mark and Ruby were the "Happy Couple."

Mark said something about how his cup runneth over, and shifted his chair a few inches away from Kit.

Ruby looked ready to scalp someone.

Mrs. Van Winterden cleared her throat delicately. "The staff here tries to make people feel at home. Good wait staff is so important. That's why I urge couples to host their reception in a five-star facility such as this whenever possible—finances permitting, of course." She turned her spectacles toward Ruby. Now it was her turn to squirm.

"I couldn't agree more," Ruby said coolly.

A waiter in black tie appeared to take their breakfast orders: oatmeal with sliced bananas for Kit, eggs hollandaise with salmon for Mark, a fresh fruit plate for Mrs. Van Winterden, and grapefruit with black coffee for Ruby.

"Kit, I've been thinking about your article and it's just the sweetest idea," Ruby began. "I think you should start by telling everyone how it was love at first sight for us. He came into The Haberdashery one day when I was working."

The Haberdashery was Madison Avenue's most elite

mens wear shop. The original was located on Jermyn Street in London, and a third shop was on Rodeo Drive in Beverly Hills. Several famous young models had been discovered working the floor of The Haberdashery.

"I had just done a photo shoot for my portfolio that morning." Ruby said. "We spent the morning shooting black and white. I don't have color yet," she said as an aside to Mrs. Van Winterden.

As though, Kit mused, Mrs. Van Winterden might be wondering if Ruby had color head shots available.

Ruby continued, "There I was, rearranging some items in the window display. Mark walked by, saw me, and came in."

"I was looking for a pay phone. I'd left my cell phone at the gym," Mark explained. Kit bit back a smile.

Ruby continued. "Anyway, there I was in the window and in walks the man who was going to rock my world. I knew right away."

Kit knew how Ruby felt.

"She talked me into buying a brown suit," Mark said.

Kit couldn't contain a laugh. Even Mrs. Van Winterden smiled.

"Darling, please," Ruby said, "nobody cares what you bought that day. And anyway, brown is the new black," she added, with a glance at Mrs. Van Winterden. "Anyway, it was really very romantic . . . how he saw me there in the window and was drawn into the store. I think it's the perfect love story. An up-and-coming Wall Street executive falls for a model struggling to make it in the Big Apple."

Struggling model? Kit glanced once more at the

David Yurman bracelets that weighed down Ruby's arms.

"Shouldn't you be writing this down?" Ruby made a scribbling motion in the air with one hand.

Kate bristled.

"Because otherwise you might leave out some of the details," Ruby said, "and it is *so* romantic." She draped a bejeweled arm across Mark.

Mark shifted in his seat. Men hated public displays of affection.

"Actually, I don't need to take notes about the way you met," Kit replied. "Based on Mrs. Van Winterden's advice, the focus of the story will be on the wedding itself—how the two of you will design the wedding of your dreams—both of you." She paused, emphasizing the word *both*,

The winning essay had focused mainly on Ruby's vision of the perfect wedding day. Family and friends, a designer gown, food and flowers—specially designed to say, "Hello, world, celebrate *us!*" The essay had been accompanied by a PowerPoint presentation virtually calling out, "Hello, judges, choose us and your magazine will sell like hotcakes!"

Ruby's entry had won her a free wedding. What was missing, it seemed, was any mention of what the groom wanted.

Mrs. Van Winterden finished chewing a mouthful of berries, put her fork down, and came to life.

"The way I see it," she said, gazing at a point somewhere in the foliage of the potted palms, "Kit's article will reinforce the advice I give in *Weddings, the Van Winterden Way.*"

Kit started writing.

"Which is to say that any couple, regardless of budget, can plan the perfect day with the help of my book."

Right. But it would, of course, help if they could spring for a place like The Palm Court, where the oatmeal cost ten bucks. Kit wrote as fast as she could, aware that Mrs. Van Winterden's tiny eyes missed nothing. She had been dubbed the "Grande Dame" of weddings by the media but around the offices of *White Weddings,* the magazine she had founded more than four decades earlier, Mrs. Van Winterden was known as "Great White," after the powerful predator that ruled the seas.

"Are we all clear on this?" Mrs. Van Winterden asked. It wasn't really a question.

"Yes," Kit replied.

"Sounds good," Mark said.

Ruby's perfect lips fell into a tiny pout. She turned her gaze to Kit. "Maybe you could add a sidebar about how we met."

Chapter Two

Weddings the Van Winterden Way: The groom should give the finest ring he can. If his budget does not allow for an adequate diamond, another precious gemstone may be substituted.

Kit wrinkled her nose in distaste. She had just read the "Page Six" gossip column in the day's *New York Post*:

> *Sources at Tiffany tell us they sold a four-carat bauble to Mark Dawson, one-half of Gotham's most in-love couple. He shopped till he dropped yesterday with his bride-to-be, Rachel Lucinda Lattingly of Great Neck, Long Island. They traded in the groom's family jewels for a pear-shaped pink diamond. Of the minute and serious bling! Tiffany is one-stop shopping for Mark and Ruby, who won a free wedding, from the dress to the*

cake. This affair of the heart will be broadcast live on Big Breakfast. *Call in late for work that day and tune in,* liebchen, *since it's being planned by the Grande Dame herself, my very good friend Ethel Van Winterden. Guess the groom decided to splurge on a new ring with all the money they're saving. It's enough to make a girl sharpen her pencil and enter a few contests, isn't it?*

Kit let out a long breath and looked across the lunch table at Edgar Lacey, *White Weddings* art director and her best friend in the world. "Unbelievable."

"I thought you'd be thrilled. They're *your* happy couple, right?"

Kit scowled. "They're the happy couple, all right. But they're not *my* happy couple. And four carats? That's not a ring—that's a weapon!"

Edgar raised an eyebrow. "Tacky? Perhaps. I'm not a fan of pear cut, as you know."

Kit smiled in spite of feeling she had been kicked in the stomach. Edgar was unusually well-versed in all things bridal.

"But you must admit," he said, tapping the newspaper with the handle of his lunch fork, "this is good for business. Your P.R. dollars at work." He took another bite.

Kit had difficulty swallowing. Her sautéed tofu and spring vegetables had turned to garden mulch in her mouth. One of the perks of the job was free lunch made with macrobiotic ingredients and served daily in a state-of-the art cafeteria designed by a team of avant garde architects. The goal was a dining experience with buzz. More important to Kit, a nutritious lunch gave her the freedom to splurge on a fast-food dinner without feeling guilty.

"It says she traded in his family jewels for a bigger ring," Edgar went on.

Kit wished he'd drop the subject. She shook her head disapprovingly.

"Okay, so she's focused on the bottom line," Edgar said, munching on his basmati rice.

Kit tried not to glare as she dumped more low-sodium soy sauce on her steamed vegetables.

"Tell me." Edgar always knew when Kit was holding something back.

"Nothing," Kit sniffed. They spent so much time together they had developed their own shorthand, which meant they could have an entire conversation using very few words. At the moment, it was annoying.

"Cookie," Edgar urged in a warning tone. It was his pet name for her.

Kit sniffed again.

"Uh-oh. Your allergies are flaring. Bad sign."

Kit suffered from allergies somehow made worse by the topic of big weddings. Strange but true. "Nothing."

"Cookie," he said again.

She shook her head, staring down at the *Post*. "It's just . . . well, what bride would turn down her husband's family jewels? That's so cold."

Edgar shrugged. "Who cares? Placements like this," he tapped the open paper, "are good for business."

"But it's his wedding, too." Kit reddened. She'd said more than she had intended.

Edgar stopped chewing and gave her a probing look. "Uh-oh."

"What?"

"You've a crush, don't you?" Edgar was English, and had a way of making things sound silly sometimes. Like now.

Kit felt her cheeks flush. She glanced around the cafeteria, hoping nobody could hear them. "Don't."

"Now Cookie, don't be embarrassed." He pushed his plate away, warming to the subject. "I know you haven't dated in a long, long time."

It *had* been a long time. Kit winced.

"But it's the most natural thing in the world. You've nothing to be embarrassed about."

Except that this was the biggest assignment of her career, the one that was going to catapult her to the rank of senior editor and get her an office with a real door and a window. She wasn't about to throw it all way for a crush on a man who was about to marry someone else. Kit pushed her plate away and looked at her friend. "I do not have a crush. And I am not embarrassed." But her red cheeks gave her away.

"One day you'll have a fine wedding of your own. And I will be there to help you plan it."

"Old ground. Let's move on, please."

"Don't worry. In good time, Cookie."

Kit sighed wearily. She had not had a steady boyfriend for ages. In fact, she couldn't even remember the last time she'd cooked dinner for a man in her apartment. The truth was, despite the fact that Kit worked for the world's number one bridal magazine, she had no prospects for a wedding of her own. Kit sniffed again.

Edgar handed her his paper napkin. He had his own theory about Kit.

She sneezed.

"Gesundheit, darling. Your parents' divorce has put you off weddings forever. Your goal in life is to be a famous journalist and never get married. But one day you will. Trust me." He smiled indulgently.

Edgar could be so annoying.

"Uncle Edgar knows all. You are going to make some lucky man the perfect wife. And, my darling, you will have the perfect wedding."

Kit sneezed into the napkin again, louder this time.

"I know, I know," Edgar said as though he was speaking to a small child. "It's a scary thought."

"Edgar, can we please let this drop?" Kit's voice was muffled by the napkin.

"All right," he said, soothingly. "You're practically a walking billboard for Benadryl. But one more thing. I know you can make it on your own."

Kit scowled.

"Come, come. No long faces. You can't afford Botox on your salary anyway."

Kit tried to muster a stern look. But he was right, as usual.

"This is your big chance, Cookie, so keep smiling. Deal?" Edgar held up one pinky finger.

Kit smiled. She wrapped her pinky around his and squeezed. "Deal."

Kit watched rain hit the dark pavement on East Fifty-fifth Street, two floors below. It had been a tough few hours. Her eyes itched, her feet ached, and she hadn't eaten anything since lunch eight hours earlier. She was standing inside the French windows of the Library at the St. Regis Hotel on her first official Happy-Couple assignment with Mrs. Van Winterden.

A local news crew was filming a segment on catering—specifically, whether the white truffle-infused chicken for which the St. Regis chef was renowned could be best enjoyed at lunch or dinner, seated or buffet. *White Weddings'* P.R. department was working round-the-clock to get as much media hype as possible for Mark and Ruby's wedding. The mere thought of it was enough to make Kit sneeze.

"Gesundheit." Mark Dawson appeared at Kit's side.

"Thanks." She sneezed again.

Mark reached into his breast pocket, pulled out a handkerchief and handed it to her.

It was a twin to the one he'd given her several days ago in the taxicab. White linen with the letter *D* embroidered in the corner. Kit buried her nose in it. "Soon I'll have the whole set."

Mark grinned. "Collect 'em all."

His smile was as big and sweet as she remembered. And in this light his eyes looked like they could melt snow. He was the same man, all right. Handsome, sexy, and engaged to be married in less than two weeks. Kit blew her nose loudly.

"This is quite a place," Mark said, motioning at the room behind them. "I read in the press kit that it was built in the early 1900s for Colonel John Jacob Astor."

A man who later went down with the Titanic, a fact Kit decided not to mention. She nodded, "His books are still on the shelves. The Library would be the perfect place for a small wedding." The words came out before she thought better of it. Kit felt the onslaught of more sniffles. Her eyes stung. She dabbed them with his handkerchief.

"Have you got a cold?" Mark leaned toward her, concerned.

The sense of him beside her in the soft light, tall and elegant in his double-breasted navy suit was enough to give a woman chills. "Nope. Allergies."

He looked at her as if this were the most interesting thing he had ever heard. "What are you allergic to?"

She tried to shrug it off. "Nothing."

"I hope it's not my aftershave." He frowned, concerned.

"No," she said quickly, "it's just . . ." There was no way to say it without sounding silly.

"What?" He leaned in closer.

He was the perfect height. Kit came to the bridge of his nose in her heels. So that if she tilted her face up she could reach his lips. Bad thought. It made her knees shake. She giggled. Nervous reaction.

He smiled, the corners of his mouth twitching playfully. "Come on, what makes you sneeze?"

"Can't."

"Tell me."

This was getting silly. Kit drew in a deep breath, and was about to confess her dark secret when Ruby's voice rang out, nearby and accusing. "Mark, what are you doing?"

Mark's shoulders bunched up. His jaw muscles clenched. "Just taking in the view."

Ruby didn't bother to look. "It's pitch dark and raining. Come on, darling, we need you for now for another run-through."

Mark gave Kit the sort of look she'd often seen on the face of the surgeon she'd dated when he was getting beeped and had to leave in the middle of dinner.

"Excuse me." Mark gave a curt nod and left.

At least this time nobody was hemorrhaging in post-op, Kit thought, as she turned to follow. She saw Mrs. Van Winterden watching her. Squaring her shoulders, she sniffed resolutely and walked over to face her boss. She might as well, there was nothing better to do now.

Great White appeared energetic and on alert, despite the fact that they'd been working for hours. She was fresh and ready to pounce.

Great White surveyed Kit. "Catering is vitally important to a successful wedding reception."

The camera lights glinted off Great White's trademark lenses obscuring her tiny, deep-set eyes. But Kit knew they were aimed at her.

"So please stay focused." Great White said with a glance at Mark, who had been ushered over to take his place atop an *X* that had been marked on the floor in masking tape.

Kit nodded. "Right." She hurried over to the table where her laptop was propped open and got busy typing. Under the file "Notes to Self," she typed, *Number one: Don't get caught chit-chatting with the groom.*

Ruby was standing next to Mark. Seeing Kit's Thinkpad open, she called out to her. "You might want to include a line or two about menu choices for a bride who's also a working fashion model. You know, something about eating light."

Kit nodded and kept typing. "Notes to Self." *Number two: Avoid scary, ambitious bride like the plague.*

Great White seated herself at a table set with crystal, china, and silver flatware.

A small cadre of St. Regis butlers bearing silver platters of steaming food waited.

At the producer's signal, Mrs. Van Winterden began speaking to the camera. "It's tempting to cut costs. But let every bride be forewarned, wedding guests never forget a bad meal."

Ruby nodded vigorously, truly grateful to be spared the indignity of serving up a lousy rubber chicken on the most important day of her life.

Mark sat with his jaw clenched, trying to appear interested.

Kit's stomach rumbled at the sight of the butlers serving food. When the taping was finished, she would interview the happy couple on their catering preferences and hopefully hit her favorite Italian place for takeout on the way home.

After what seemed like ages, the producer signaled it was a wrap. The production crew gathered its equipment and vanished in a New York minute. Mrs. Van Winterden took off in search of her limo, followed by a posse of St. Regis butlers lugging her belongings.

Kit checked her notes. If she hurried, she could finish her questions with the happy-couple and be eating her takeout food in less than an hour.

One look at them brought a change in plans. They were alone at the table. Ruby was whispering furiously into Mark's ear, two bright spots of color on her flawless cheeks. Mark stared down at the white linen tablecloth. She wasn't murmuring sweet nothings, Kit decided. She could conduct her interview another time.

She grabbed her briefcase and raincoat and left. She could do the interview another time. By phone. Preferably long distance.

She reached the white marble lobby and headed out the massive brass revolving door, helped by a push from the white-gloved doorman. About to step into a waiting cab, she realized she had left her laptop upstairs. She debated whether to retrieve it tomorrow, by which time Happy Couple would have finished their argument. But the laptop was property of *White Weddings*, and had several pages of incriminatory notes stored on it.

Kit turned and headed back inside. She took the elevator up to the Library and paused before entering. It was quiet. A good sign. She walked in, spotted the laptop exactly where she'd left it, and gave a sigh of relief. Then she saw something that stopped her in her tracks.

Mark Dawson. Dining all alone.

Chapter Three

Weddings, the Van Winterden Way: A romantic dinner à deux works wonders to relieve stress during wedding preparations.

M ark sprang to his feet almost before Kit stepped into the room.

Ever the gentleman, she thought. *And dining alone in one of the most exclusive spots in New York City.*

"Ruby had to go," he said as if he could read Kit's mind. "And I couldn't let all this food go to waste. Join me." He pulled out a chair. "Please."

Kit hesitated.

"I'm starved. You must be, too."

He was right. Kit took in a deep breath, filling her lungs with the aroma of fresh roasted chicken and something else. It was the deep, warm pleasure of finding herself alone with him. She stood where she was while she considered whether it was right to join him. *A*

26

little research for her article couldn't hurt, she thought. "The chef here is known for his white truffles," she said.

"That settles it," Mark said with a grin. He pulled a Louis XIV chair out from the table set with enough gleaming silver and cut-crystal stemware to qualify for a photo shoot in *Town & Country.*

Candles twinkled and a real wood fire burned merrily away in the fireplace. Kit nodded.

Mark closed the few steps between them in a flash, taking her coat from her before the butler had a chance.

Kit was intensely aware of Mark's hands on her shoulders. She felt his breath on her neck and a tingle ran down her back. He waved the butler away, helping her into her chair. He pushed her gently into place at the small table. Not too close and not too far away. Just right. He was knocking off those Van Winterden rules of etiquette one by one. A girl could get used to this.

"Ruby had to drop off proofs of her head shots downtown," Mark said. "For her modeling portfolio."

"Oh," Kit said, as if she understood completely. Except she didn't. Ruby had left Mark, the most handsome man on earth, to eat his dinner alone in the St. Regis hotel, on a rainy night.

The butler returned, filling their plates with steaming food. Kit watched Mark settle back into his chair and let out a long, deep breath, as though he had been waiting to exhale all night. He slowly ran one hand across his jaw. He had a five o'clock shadow. Sexy.

His eyes looked warmer and bigger than ever in this light. He watched her, his gaze never straying, as the

butler finished his task and disappeared down the hall.
A girl could get lost in those eyes, and not even mind.
She was glad she had worn her favorite ivory silk
blouse, as she felt pretty in it. That thought, along with
the feel of Mark's gaze upon her, made her self-
conscious. "This smells good," she said, feeling her
cheeks flush.

"Pretty much the same thing I'd be having at my
place," Mark said with a twinkle in his eye.

Kit giggled, feeling more at ease.

"Bon apetit." Mark held his glass aloft. Kit reached
for hers and they made a toast. "Or, as we say at my
place, dig in."

Kit needed no urging. Dinner was delicious. Spring
chicken, slow-roasted, seasoned with white truffles,
and served with ragout of baby vegetables. They fell
into a comfortable silence and sampled everything on
their plates.

"I'd say Mrs. Van Winterden knows her stuff," Mark
said between bites.

Kit nodded, feeling something she hadn't felt in a
very long time. The feeling, she realized, was one of
complete contentment.

Mark watched her from across the table with a smile
that mirrored her own. "It is vitally important," he
whispered in a perfect falsetto, "that the bride and
groom find a chef with at least one Michelin star to
cater their reception. Don't you agree, Ms. McCabe?"

It was a pitch-perfect imitation of Great White's
whispery voice. Kit giggled. "I do indeed, Mrs. Van
Winterden."

"Because otherwise," Mark held an imaginary book

in one hand and pointed to it with a tiny fluttering motion, "the guests will be fed up. No pun intended."

Kit laughed so hard she had to put her fork down.

Mark frowned and pursed his lips. The resemblance was uncanny, all things considered. "Quite."

Kit leaned back in her chair, now helpless with laughter. "And the wedding will be doomed." Poor choice of words, she realized too late. The laughter died in her throat, and the words hung between them.

Mark grew quiet as well. He gave his head a small shake as if to rid his mind of an unwelcome thought.

Kit winced. They were the perfect couple on paper, with flawless pedigrees and even rent-controlled apartments in the right section of town. But in person they were different from their image, somehow.

Mark's smile was tinged with sadness as he quickly changed the subject. "Admit it. You came back for the chow. A lot of women don't enjoy a good meal. But this," he waved his hand over the table, "is amazing."

Kit blushed. Judging from the looks of Ruby—all ninety pounds of her—he probably didn't often see a woman enjoying a meal. Kit had always envied tall, willowy women who were content to order a salad with dressing on the side. She just was not one of them. "I was famished," she admitted.

Mark chuckled. "Me, too. I'm ready for seconds."

As if on cue, the butler appeared, restocked Mark's plate, and disappeared. Mark took another bite. "Wow. This is fantastic."

Kit nodded. "The chef here really did earn his Michelin star for his use of white truffles. Lucky for us they're in season."

Mark raised an eyebrow. "There's a season for white truffles?"

"You bet. I spent my junior year in Provence," Kit explained with a smile.

Mark considered this, beaming at her. He raised his glass. "I'm impressed. It's not often I have the opportunity to dine with a famous magazine editor who also knows when white truffles are in season. I propose a toast. To you."

Kit felt her cheeks redden.

"Hey, I'm not teasing," he said softly, seriously. "I moved to New York just after college, expecting to meet the most interesting and sophisticated women. But I have discovered they're few and far between." A shadow crossed his face.

"You only need to meet one. And you have," Kit added quickly, hoisting her glass. Poor Mark. He was about to marry a woman who seemed more concerned that the photographs capture her best angle than with whether her fiancé likes the way the wedding is shaping up.

Mark took a sip of his wine and dropped his gaze to the spotless linen tablecloth, his jaw tightening slowly.

"Planning a wedding is a tough job," Kit said, trying to comfort him. What she wanted to do was warn him to get out now, while there was still time. But she couldn't bear to see him sad. And besides, she reminded herself, her job was to report on his wedding, not talk him out of it. "I'm sure things will lighten up soon. There's the honeymoon to look forward to."

"Yeah, of course," Mark said, looking at her thoughtfully. "Still, I want to propose another toast." He lifted his glass. "To the only woman I've ever met who knows when white truffles are in season."

Kit felt her heart melt. She raised her glass with a none-too-steady hand and looked at the handsome man across the table. He was charming, intelligent, kind, and sweet. But he was about to be married. A big *but*. Kit searched for something—anything—to get the conversation back onto a professional track. She fell back on an old favorite. "So, where'd you spend your junior year abroad?"

He shook his head. "I didn't go abroad till after I graduated. Then I joined the Peace Corps. I spent a year in the Dominican Republic."

Now it was Kit's turn to be impressed. "Good for you. I always wanted to serve in the Peace Corps. I just didn't get around to it." The truth was, she had been so anxious to begin building her career that she had accepted a job and started work three days after graduation, before she even had a chance to unpack. She had wanted to feel settled, and hoped a steady job would help.

"I like to help people," Mark said. "I'm told I do that to a fault." This time there was no mistaking the sadness in his face.

Kit knew without asking that his big heart was what got him into trouble.

Mark sat quietly, shaking his head as if to clear his mind. "So, I learned a lot tonight. I've never seen a news segment being filmed. I guess you're used to that sort of thing, working with Mrs. Van Winterden."

Kit gave a small nod. She didn't tell him that except for an annual appearance at the company party, the closest she came to Great White was an occasional sighting in the "Sunday Styles" pages of *The New York Times*. "This was my first time, too. It was interesting." Until about the fifth take, when her stomach had started rumbling for dinner.

"I'm glad they finally got it to turn out all right," Mark said. "That's the important thing. And Ruby enjoyed it."

Which is to say, Kit thought, *Mark had not.*

"She's learning a lot from these press events. We both are," Mark said, twirling the stem of his wine goblet with one hand. A muscular hand.

The sight of it sent a shiver down her spine. She remembered reading in the contest entry that he was an expert kayaker with a national ranking. Strong hands. Strong shoulders, too, probably.

"She's hoping all this publicity from the magazine contest will help her get started in modeling."

The words landed like so many small rocks hitting a pool of water, each one marring the surface. One of the dumbest reasons anyone could have for getting married, in Kit's mind, was to use the wedding to get a modeling career off the ground. She couldn't say that, however. She lifted her glass to buy time while she thought of something to say. She studied it for spots (there were none) and took a sip.

Mark watched her. "I guess it sounds a little crazy, huh?"

Yes, Kit thought. "This will be an exciting time," she said. It occurred to her that Mark was the sort of person who couldn't say no. To be fair, Ruby looked the type who didn't take no for an answer. Kit took another sip of wine.

"Yeah," Mark replied with a small shrug. "We would have gotten engaged anyway, even without the contest. Sooner or later."

Now his words were landing like boulders, each setting off its own large ring of waves. Kit stared at Mark while his words sunk in. "Huh?"

Mark reddened. He grimaced and ran his fingers around the collar of his shirt as though it had grown too tight around his neck. He unbuttoned the collar button and yanked savagely at his tie. "We had talked about getting engaged . . . eventually."

Kit's jaw dropped. She snapped it shut and nodded as though she understood completely—Except that she didn't. "Uh-huh," she murmured.

"But then Ruby entered this contest and . . . ," Mark's voice trailed off.

The boulders were now setting off waves the size of a tsunami. Kit shook her head to clear it of disastrous images. She tried to remind herself that he was a client and this was about business, after all. "And now you're on the fast track to wedded bliss," Kit finished the sentence for him.

Mark gave a tight smile. "Yeah. It's every bride's dream, right?"

Kit gave a small shrug. The thought of a big wedding, complete with Ethel Van Winterden whispering stage directions into a tiny microphone on the big day, was enough to bring on a case of sniffles for Kit. She dabbed her nose with the hankie he'd given her earlier.

Across the table, Mark grinned. "Glad that's coming in handy. Hey, you never told me what you're allergic to."

Kit looked down, blushing.

"You promised," Mark reminded her.

When she looked up at him, his eyes looked soft and sweet. She felt she could tell him her silliest secret and he would not laugh. She took a deep breath. "I'm allergic to weddings." It was only a half-truth. Edgar would have said it was fear of commitment. But what did he know? "Every time I get near a formal china pattern, or all those floral arrangements, I just feel it coming on," Kit explained. Her eyes began to water at the mere mention of these things.

"Engraved invitations?" Mark asked, watching her with interest.

Kit nodded, feeling her throat start to tighten. She felt a wheeze in her lungs. She gave small cough and nodded.

"Bridesmaids' dresses?" Mark watched her with interest. His eyes now were definitely twinkling.

Kit gave another small cough.

Mark chuckled and shook his head. "I thought it was just a guy thing." He handed her a glass of water. "It must be a real hazard, considering where you work. At least a guy only has to go through this once."

If he is lucky. Their eyes met in a knowing glance and Kit was certain he was thinking it, too. She shuddered. It was awful. He wasn't even married, and she was already planning his divorce. "It would be bad for business if Mrs. Van Winterden found out," she said finally.

"I see," Mark said solemnly. "Your secret's safe with me."

And yours, Kit thought, *is safe with me.*

"Here's to getting through this," he said, raising his glass.

Kit solemnly clinked her glass with his.

"Chin up, Kit."

She liked hearing him say her name. She watched him take a sip of wine and swallow, his Adam's apple bobbing up and down a couple times. His lips looked very full. The observation brought on another tingle deep inside that made her shiver and filled her head with one single, powerful thought. What would it be like to be with a man who looked at her like that?

Wonderful. Beyond my wildest dreams. Kit smiled. For the first time in her entire life she felt she could be happy forever with the man sitting across the table from her. In some crazy way Kit was happy to simply know that somewhere in the great, wide world there was a man she could fall for, head over heels, just the way she had always heard it should be. The realization rushed through her with the heat and intensity of an electric current, and it pushed every other thought out of her mind.

Mark smiled back at her as though he felt it, too.

Chapter Four

Weddings, the Van Winterden Way: Invite family and good friends to join the festivities.

Mark Dawson felt a warm glow take hold somewhere deep inside him and spread through his entire being. He'd never felt like this. His heart danced even as he stood, being fitted for a suit. He shifted his weight impatiently from one foot to the other.

"Just a moment longer Mr. Dawson, please." The tailor was growing impatient.

But Mark couldn't hold still. Kit was near. The sight of her made him want to push the tailor away, jump down, and run after her, even though he knew he shouldn't be feeling this way about her. He tried to push his feelings aside—a task made no easier by the bad behavior of his oldest and best friend who was standing at his side.

Chip Beaupre let out a low whistle and grinned.

That did it. Mark forgot all about the stirring in his solar plexus and focused on Chip, wondering if he could still take him in a fight. He turned his head and studied Chip, eyes narrowing. They were the same size as they had been in high school—plus or minus ten pounds. Chip Beaupre was an inch taller than Mark, but slower.

"She's hot. Definitely looks as good going as she does coming," Chip whispered, his gaze glued to Kit McCabe's derriere.

Mark had to admit, Kit did look hot in her tailored gray pants. She wore a fetching pink sweater that showed off her curves and highlighted her red hair tumbling loose and free around her shoulders. Very sexy. The heat inside Mark turned up a notch.

Chip whistled. Low, but loud enough for everyone to hear—as though he were back in the locker room at high school, rather than taping a TV segment in the formal menswear department on the sixth floor of Saks Fifth Avenue.

Kit ducked her head and blushed like a schoolgirl.

Mark glared at Chip.

"Hey, buddy, you're practically hitched already," Chip said with a leer. "Leave some for the rest of us."

Mark scowled. *Men could be such pigs,* he thought, startling himself.

"What's her story?" Chip motioned toward Kit with his chin.

"She's trying to do her job. Her boss," Mark glanced toward Mrs. Van Winterden, "is being filmed to promote her new book."

Chip shrugged and continued watching Kit. "She's still hot."

Mark grimaced. "The last thing she needs," he whispered evenly, "is a guy like you." Chip had cheated on every girl he had ever dated, starting with his date for the junior prom. He was, from the female point of view, a snake.

"I'll be the judge of that," Chip whispered, grinning.

"Not likely," Mark said hoarsely through clenched teeth. The last thing a sweet girl like Kit McCabe needed was a guy like Chip. *Woman,* he corrected himself. Kit was mature and intelligent. Definitely a woman. Not a girl. Mark opened his mouth to say so, but thought better of it. From the looks of things, Chip did not need any encouragement. "You should back off."

"No worries," Chip whispered with a grin. "I can handle this one on my own. Using the Beaupre method, tried and true."

Mark shot him a severe look. Chip had been his friend since the third grade, and had agreed to be best man at his wedding the weekend after next—to Ruby. The thought made Mark painfully aware of the straight pins digging into his arms and legs like dozens of tiny daggers. He felt trapped, pinned down like Gulliver. Tugging at his collar, he drew in a deep breath. "This is taking forever."

"Easy, big guy, we'll be done soon." Chip patted Mark on the shoulder. "And in the meantime, relax and enjoy the view." He turned his gaze once again to Kit, who had just reentered the room, toting an easel and giant poster-sized cover of Mrs. Van Winterden's new book.

Kit looked incredibly sexy, and Mark could not take

his eyes off her. He felt his blood heat up again, which made the scratching of the straight pins seem even worse. He felt beads of sweat forming on his chest. Again he shifted his weight and sighed.

Kit stopped to arrange the easel, bending forward and providing a great view of her curves. It was too much.

Mark stepped off the tailor's platform and strode quickly over to Kit, ignoring the straight pins that ripped into his legs at every step. He leaned in close to her, aware of her sweet scent—something floral, gardenia maybe. He breathed in deeply. "Let me give you a hand," he said, reaching for the easel.

Not to be outdone, Chip quickly trotted across the fitting room. He was beside them in a flash. He reached for the poster board and tried to tuck it under one arm. Then he reached for the easel. "I've got this."

Kit smiled, murmuring something about chivalry being alive and well.

Her voice tinkled like music to Mark's ears, unleashing something inside him that made him dizzy. He felt his lips break into a grin that he feared would split his face in two. The top of her head came up to the bridge of his nose. She was the perfect height for him. Ruby was six feet tall, and complained often that she couldn't wear heels around him. Mark could not stop smiling at Kit. He felt himself draw closer to her. He gave a small tug on the easel. "I've got it."

Kit kept on smiling. Mark felt like a knight in shining armor. She was adorable, no doubt about it. Especially at close range. The bright lights of the dressing room brought out the gold highlights in her hair and the green in her eyes. The sight dazzled him, and his stomach fluttered. He liked the feeling. Suddenly, he no longer minded the fact that he had spent the last hour posing as a human pin cushion.

"I can take it," Chip said, giving another sharp tug on the easel.

Mark yanked back. "No problem. I got it."

Chip tightened his grip. "It's okay."

Mark looked at his friend, eyes narrowing. He was aware the room had grown quiet. They were being childish. But he couldn't help himself. He'd always assumed that when he got married, he would stop noticing other women. But his wedding was barely two weeks away and he was noticing this woman. Big time. This was not how things were supposed to be. Mark let go of the easel.

The sudden release sent Chip reeling backwards a few steps. He recovered his balance and stood, easel in hand. "Thanks." He shot Mark a quizzical look. "I think."

That night, Mark tossed and turned in bed, unable to sleep. After the filming had ended, he and Chip had met Ruby for dinner in Chinatown, that maze of streets near the Brooklyn Bridge. They had settled into a booth and ordered. Of course Chip had steered the conversation to Kit McCabe, and whether Ruby thought he should ask her out.

"Brilliant!" Ruby had exclaimed. "Then we can double-date."

Mark's mooshoo pork turned to ashes in his mouth.

Chip grinned like the Cheshire cat.

Mark scowled.

"Pay no attention to him," Ruby said, picking at her steamed vegetables with a fork. "He's been grumpy all day. You can see it on the tape. He looks as grumpy as a grizzly bear."

She turned to Mark. "Seriously, darling," she continued, "you need to keep a positive attitude during these P.R. events. A lot is riding on this." She paused to see if Mark was listening.

He had not noticed until now that she had a habit of speaking with her mouth full.

Ruby chewed quickly, warming to her subject. "If we play our cards right, who knows what it could do for my career? Look at all the people who've become famous after appearing on reality TV shows. Most of them aren't even attractive, and now you read about them in every issue of *People* magazine." Ruby leaned across the table, frowning. "Please try to remember, darling, lots of agents might tune in to watch our wedding. And nobody wants to see a grumpy groom."

Her words rang in Mark's head hours later, as he rolled over and punched his pillows. But sleep wouldn't come. His wedding was fast approaching. This was supposed to be the happiest time in his life, wasn't it? His heart raced. Sleep was impossible.

Kit's face filled his mind. Dining with her by candlelight, and seeing her again today, knowing she was up for grabs with other men, had made his heart skip a beat. His father had warned him about this. Every marriage went through tough times, eventually. "Special challenges," his father had called them. Times when another woman might catch his eye or pop into his thoughts. At such times sports were a good thing in a man's life, his father had said. His father was practically a scratch golfer. Their den at home in Michigan was chock full of trophies.

But what if the woman in question caught his eye *before* the wedding had even occurred? What if she did more than catch his eye? What if she was smart and funny and unbelievably sexy? What if every time he closed his eyes and tried to sleep, it was Kit's face he saw in the dark, not Ruby's?

Chapter Five

Weddings, the Van Winterden Way: The exchange of vows is a deeply personal and spiritual expression of the couple's shared beliefs.

Several days passed in a haze of happiness. Without quite knowing it, Kit felt she was floating through time on a cushion of soft air. She found herself trading smiles with strangers, making jokes at work and truly enjoying her free time. She replayed her conversations with Mark many times, and saw his face whenever she closed her eyes. She was almost able to kid herself that she was just enjoying her new assignment. Almost.

She had quite a surprise the day they were taping the segment on wedding vows. Suddenly, it had become harder to think of Mark without thinking of Ruby and her super-sized diamond ring. In fact, Kit's dinner with Mark at the St. Regis seemed a long way off on the morning she found herself standing in front of a church on Fifth Avenue, one of the most famous stretches of sidewalk in the world. It was precisely the spot where countless brides-to-be had stood, including famous movie starlets, a former First Lady, and even a real princess. And, in less than two weeks, Ruby Lattingly Dawson's name would be added to the list.

Kit gazed up, as the others must have, at the field-stone façade of the venerable Mid-Manhattan Church. It was cool and gray in the pre-dawn light. She knew he was there, inside. Waiting. Ready to recite the vows that would change their lives forever.

Her heart beat like a jackhammer, and she scolded herself for it. She was here to take notes, nothing more.

The sound of cooing reached Kit's ears. She looked up to see a pair of morning doves nesting high above. An omen, her mother would say. A symbol the world over of two people in love. Kit shivered.

Kit drained the last of her double espresso and tossed the empty cup into a trash bin on the avenue. The caffeine had done nothing to calm the emotions that were twisting through her heart like a tornado. She did her best to ignore them as she climbed the granite steps of the famous old church.

The happy couple's segment on wedding vows would air tomorrow on *Big Breakfast*. The coming week would be a whirlwind of events, including their engagement party, in preparation for the big day.

The thought of watching Mark and Ruby exchange vows, even pretend vows, was enough to tighten the knot in Kit's stomach. She shivered, chalking it up to the cool morning air. Taking a deep breath and pulling open the giant oak door, she entered the church, blinking as her eyes adjusted to the dim light inside.

The door swung shut behind her with a soft click. She stood still, taking in the silence. A faint odor of incense hung in the air, tickling her nose until she felt a telltale sniffle start to brew. She entered the central nave of the gigantic church. Row upon row of polished oak pews lined with crimson cushions stretched out before her, leading to an immense altar of polished white marble. Dust motes danced in the first rays of morning sunlight that had worked their way in through stained glass windows, making Kit's nose twitch even more.

In the distance the altar hummed with activity. The *Big Breakfast* production crew was at work, taping down electrical wires and stringing lights. Mrs. Van Winterden stood to one side, as a sound technician wired a microphone to the front of her suit, which was mother-of-the-bride blue satin.

Mark was there. She sensed him even before she saw him, standing still as a statue at the top of the short flight of steps leading up to the altar. The sight of him gave her heart a jolt. He was tall and strikingly handsome, even at this distance.

She felt his gaze on her, scanning her from head to toe. It heightened the soft feel of her knit dress against her skin, which was now tingling. She reached down unconsciously and drew her trench coat belt tighter around her waist as she walked toward him.

A yearning rose from deep inside her, like a bubbling pool of warm water. It mixed with her happiness at seeing him again. She looked at his face, from the deep brown eyes to the dimple in his chin, and realized with a rush he was more handsome than she remembered. It took her breath away, and made her feel like she was again walking on that cushion of air.

"Hi," he mouthed the word from across the nave.

"Hi," she felt her face break into a big, wide smile. No Ruby in sight, either. This was good. But the thought brought a pang, reminding her that Mark was spoken for, and she looked away.

The producer of *Big Breakfast* caught sight of Kit and raced over to her. "Thank goodness you're here. I need you. Ten minutes to air and no bride in sight." He studied his clipboard, grabbed her arm, and began steering her up the aisle. "We need a body to do a sound check and light reading. *Now.* Up on the altar. You can practice being a bride," he said, with a quick smile.

Kit gulped, dabbing at the dampness that had suddenly sprung up in her eyes. Thank goodness for the tissue she always kept tucked inside one sleeve—not to mention waterproof mascara. She followed the producer up the center aisle, trying to concentrate on what he was saying. But all she could think of was Mark.

He waited at the altar, watching her approach with shining eyes. Maybe it was just the reflection of the twinkling candles that had been lit all around to lend atmosphere for the shot. Kit couldn't be sure.

He rubbed one hand through his hair.

He must be nervous, too, she thought.

She drew closer and he smiled slowly, deliberately and wide. The smile lit up his face from the inside out.

Kit felt like she had won first place at the state fair and got to take him home as the prize.

When he spoke, his voice was husky and deep. "Hi, Kit." His Adam's apple bobbed with the effort.

The sound of that voice saying her name sent a jolt of pure, electric pleasure through Kit's veins. Her name had never sounded so wonderful on anyone else's lips. It took her breath away. Her voice, when it came out, was barely more than a whisper. "Hi."

He smiled.

Kit smiled back.

Mark's brown eyes shone even brighter.

Kit felt her knees go soft.

The producer was busy directing his staff. Kit tried to follow what he was saying, but her eyes kept returning to Mark. He looked tall and lean, more handsome than ever in his navy suit and silk tie of pale yellow. It set off his eyes.

She wondered what it would be like to stand here at the altar for real and exchange vows with this man, to give herself to him forever. The thought made a flush of heat rise up from deep within. Her cheeks turned hot.

Kit reminded herself this was just a dry run. And that Mark would soon do it for real with someone else.

"Good morning, Ms. McCabe." Great White had appeared soundlessly from the dimness and was suddenly beside them. She was wired for sound, and ready for business. Her trademark spectacles were trained on Kit. "We're depending on you to keep us on track this morning."

Kit gave a small nod. They were in dire straits if they were depending on her to stay on track because she felt shaky and not at all steady. Mark Dawson always seemed to have this effect on her. She stood still while a sound technician attached a cordless microphone pack around her waist, hoping the equipment would not pick up the sound of her heart thumping inside her chest.

The producer consulted his clipboard and rattled off a list of items they needed to cover, beginning with a sound check.

It was Mark's turn next, and Kit was aware of his gaze on her while he was being fitted for his microphone. She almost swooned when he unbuttoned his jacket so the battery pack could be attached to his belt. She forced herself to look away and tried to will her cheeks to cool down. She was certain they were flaming with heat.

The producer directed Kit and Mark to step up to the altar and take their places at the top. He waved everyone else away as Kit took the shallow steps slowly, aware of Mark's hand resting on the small of her back. The weight of it sent a jolt of excitement through her.

She stood facing Mark, as bright lights were switched on, shutting out any view of the immense church around them and giving the illusion that they were alone together in the vast space.

"Step closer together, you two," the producer called.

Kit stood rooted to the spot. She didn't trust her legs to move.

Mark took a step closer to her, bringing his face within inches of hers.

The smell his woodsy aftershave filled her. Kit felt as if she was on top of a high dive, about to fly off into a perfect swan dive. Her eyes met his. They were warm, dark pools—the kind a woman wanted to swim in forever.

"Let's start, people," the producer said. "Kit, step in. I want you to look at each other as though you mean it."

Kit felt every muscle in her body working in precision, as though she were flying. She took a step closer to Mark, felt the heat of him coming at her in waves. She sensed the hardness of his body through his suit, coiled tightly, ready for action. Again she felt a rush of warmth from head to toe.

Mark cleared his throat. He smiled.

She smiled back.

"Time for sound checks," the producer called. "We'll start with you, Mark. Say whatever comes to mind."

His gaze steady, Mark began to speak. His voice strong and smooth. " 'My beloved is like a gazelle or a young stag,' " he began.

The words thrilled Kit as though she was hearing them for the first time. In fact, Mark was quoting from "Song of Solomon," probably the most popular lines from the Old Testament for a wedding. Today the words sounded new to her ears, each going straight to her heart. Kit felt the smile on her face grow even wider as Mark continued to speak.

The church grew quiet around them, as though even the production crew had fallen under a spell. Except for the faint cooing of doves somewhere out of sight, high above, silence surrounded them.

The giant room seemed to spin slowly around Kit. She stood rooted to the spot, transfixed by the sound of Mark's voice. His words washed over her. She wished the moment could last forever. As Mark continued to speak, Kit forgot about the other people in the room, forgot she had no business allowing herself to feel this way, forgot he belonged to someone else. She felt her body slowly shift itself into perfect alignment with his, until she was leaning in close to him, feeling his breath upon her face, drawing the scent of him into her lungs with each breath. It was a heady feeling.

Mark took one of Kit's hands in his to steady her.

His touch sent excitement rippling through Kit. Skin tingling, her entire body was poised. She longed to move one step closer, closing the gap between them. But she didn't dare.

Mark's face was just inches away from hers. His eyes *were* shining now. His jaw muscles relaxed and his lips were full. He finished speaking and watched her, his lips dangerously close to hers.

The moment was shattered by the sound of a familiar voice from the front pew. It was cool as ice and just as brittle. "I'm here."

Kit's blood ran cold.

Mark stiffened.

Ruby had arrived.

Kit came hurtling back to reality like the space shuttle during reentry. She fell fast and landed with a splash.

Mark backed away from Kit, his jaw tightening as Ruby marched up to the altar and gave him a swift peck before turning her icy gaze on Kit.

Kit swiftly unclipped her microphone, slipped off the power pack, and handed them over without a word.

One of Ruby's nails grazed the inside of Kit's wrist. Kit made a mental note to check later for blood.

Ruby's pale blue eyes glittered in a way that made Kit glad they weren't alone in a dark alley. "Looks like someone's been trying to fill my shoes."

Kit felt as though she had been slapped. Her cheeks blazed as she gave a small, miserable shake of her head. She was painfully aware that her boss and the production crew were watching them.

"Ruby," Mark said softly.

Kit took a step back. Every instinct she had told her to run. She hadn't noticed till now just how tall Ruby was. She was six feet if she was an inch. Not a comforting thought, at the moment.

Kit was saved with the help of a most unlikely source.

"Miss Lattingly, how lovely that you've arrived so we can tape our segment this morning," Mrs. Van Winterden's voice was whispery but carried a reprimand. One of the primary Van Winterden rules of etiquette was never, *ever,* be late.

Ruby stopped dead in her tracks.

Kit practically fainted with relief, and took the opportunity to make her escape. She slipped into the shadows and relative safety of a nearby pew, flipping open her laptop. She created a new file heading, "How to Recognize When You're Falling for the Wrong Man."

Her stomach did flip-flops as she watched Mark on the altar, nodding wordlessly as the producer instructed him to take a step closer to Ruby.

Mark did so, taking Ruby's hands in his. The sight sent a dagger of jealousy into Kit's stomach, which began to churn.

The producer gave a signal for the camera to roll.

Kit watched Mrs. Van Winterden give her lead-in about the various ways a couple could choose to declare their undying love for each other.

Ruby draped her arms across Mark's, and the sight churned up Kit's stomach still further. She now knew what was meant by the expression that jealousy was a "green-eyed monster." She could practically see a dragon, flames shooting from its mouth, breathing down her neck.

At the altar, Ruby explained to the camera that she and Mark would write their own vows for their big day.

Didn't they know it was the tackiest thing in the world to write their own vows? So much so that Edgar had put it at the top of his list, "Ten Signs the Marriage is Headed for Divorce." Kit's stomach took one more sickening lurch as the dragon exhaled again, unleashing a black, sooty cloud.

"Nobody can describe our love better than we can." Ruby explained into the camera.

Kit suddenly felt dizzy. The sides of the church began to swirl around her as she took a deep breath and gasped for air. But all she got was dragon breath. Her throat closed. She wheezed and doubled over in a fit of coughs. Loud, hacking coughs.

The producer held up his hand to stop the tape, turned to her and frowned.

Kit grabbed a tissue and held it to her mouth in an attempt to stifle her coughs. But it was no use. She could not stop. The sound of coughing filled the vast space, echoing all around. Tears sprang to her eyes and rolled down her cheeks. And still she coughed.

When she finally came up for air, she saw Mrs. Van Winterden staring at her with pursed lips.

Ruby eyed her from the altar with a look that gave meaning to the phrase, "icy daggers."

The corners of Mark's mouth seemed to twitch, but her eyes were so watery Kit couldn't be certain.

She struggled to find her voice. "Allergies," she mumbled thickly. For one awful moment she was afraid she would collapse in a crumpled heap on one of the polished oak pews of the world-famous Mid-Manhattan Church. Directly in front of the diva of wedding planners, her majordomo boss. Not to mention the sadly not-meant-to-be love of her life and his very, very ticked off bride-in-training. And the production staff of *Big Breakfast,* contracted to film the entire affair as part of the biggest marketing promotion in the history of *White Weddings* magazine.

Kit decided to get out of there fast. She cleared her throat with one final wheeze. "Sorry," she called. She gathered her belongings and fled the way someone runs from a burning building.

As she headed for the exit, Kit had a terrible fear that her coughing fit was probably also sounding the death knell of her career at *White Weddings*.

One look back at Great White's face confirmed this theory. But Kit could not take any more. She hurled herself against the big oak doors and ran out.

* * *

That night, Kit tossed and turned, unable to sleep, as images of the day played through her mind. She did not want to admit it, but meeting Mark Dawson had melted something deep inside her—something that had been frozen a long time ago. Even now the thought of him made her feel warm, tingly, and alive.

But the knowledge that he was about to marry some-one else was maddening. And it was taking all the fun out of her assignment. Until recently, Kit's job meant everything in the world to her. She fluffed her pillows, but it did not help her rest any easier.

Finally she gave up trying to get to sleep and switched on the lamp. The light glowed softly on walls painted a pale shade of green like dried Sea Moss.

A "restful color," Edgar called it, for a place where nothing ever happens. It was true. Most nights, she was content to work late and grab a quick dinner on the way home. And tonight she was more grateful than ever for the comfort of her small apartment. It was her sanctuary.

The phone rang, startling her. Kit checked her watch. Almost midnight. Edgar had a hot date tonight so there was only one person it could possibly be.

Kit picked up the phone. "Hi, mom," she said with-out bothering to check caller ID.

"Glad to know you recognize my ring, all the way from Asia," her mother said, laughing.

"How are things in Katmandu?"

"Stellar, my sweet baby. I'm making real progress. There is a definite loosening in the blockage to my third chakra. Dalai says I'm on the verge of a major breakthrough."

Major breakdown was more like it. Kit rolled her eyes.

On the other side of the world, her mother sensed it. "Don't make that face, sweet baby girl. I'm doing important work. The Lama says we need to use our time wisely to prepare for passage to the next level."

Kit nodded. She was well versed in the teachings of her mother's spiritual guide. She had even met him once, at his ashram outside her mother's home near Taos, New Mexico. Kit's parents divorced when she was thirteen, putting an end to the happy childhood she had spent on a ranch outside Aspen, Colorado. Kit spent her teen years shuttling between her father's new home and new wife in Los Angeles, and her mother's New York City apartment. Once Kit headed off to university, her mother gave up her apartment and set out on a spiritual quest Which led her each spring to Nepal, where she joined other members of her ashram to hike the Himalayas while the rhododendrons were in full bloom.

"So," her mother said, "what's going on there in old New York?"

Things in old New York were a bit too interesting, at the moment, Kit thought. She filled her mother in on her newest assignment, careful to leave out the part about how she was falling for the groom.

"Congratulations," her mother said when Kit was finished. "Sounds like you got exactly what you've been waiting for."

And then some, Kit thought. Mark Dawson was so wonderful he took her breath away. He was funny, intelligent and kind. Kit practically melted each time he looked at her. Standing at the altar today had, for the first time in her life, made her want to be someone's bride. But reality had set in when Ruby arrived, grabbed his arm and hung on as though she'd been born to it. Kit let out a weary sigh.

"I heard that," her mother said. "There's something you're not telling me."

Sometimes her mother acted just like everybody else's mother.

"Nothing major," Kit began. "It's just that the assignment is a little more complicated than I thought."

"How so?"

Kit stared up the ceiling, as if the right words might be written there. They weren't. "It's just that the couple who won the free wedding are getting married for all the wrong reasons."

Her mother gave a small chuckle, the kind she always made when she was about to give a life lesson.

Kit twirled a section of her hair, waiting.

"There are plenty of reasons to get married. Nobody can really judge them except for the couple getting married."

This was true. But Ruby was using her wedding to get free publicity for her modeling career. "I suppose what I meant to say, is they just seem all wrong for each other."

There was a pause at the other end of the line as her mother considered this. "Are they?"

Kit pictured her mother, sitting in her cabin in the Himalayas or wherever she was. Waiting for Kit to see the light about how her attitude needed adjustment. Kit rolled her eyes again. It was not easy having an acolyte for a mom.

"It's just that she's not his type." Kit knew she sounded defensive. "Mark is wonderful. I mean really, really special, inside and out. I can't believe I've just met him, and he's getting married." Kit felt her voice break. There, she had said it. The truth.

There was a long pause as her mother considered this.

"I almost wish I hadn't gotten this assignment," Kit added. She felt hot tears struggling to come out.

When her mother spoke, her voice sounded like a hug from halfway around the world. "Everything is happening exactly the way it's meant to happen. If you feel strongly about Mark, it's because you were meant to meet him—even if he *is* engaged. Learn what you need to, do the best you can on your assignment, and trust the universe."

Lama wisdom. Yuck. Kit opened her mouth to say it wasn't fair that she had finally met the man of her dreams only to watch him—in fact, help him—walk down the aisle with someone else. But she knew better. She snapped her mouth shut.

"More will be revealed, Sweetie. You'll see."

Kit took a deep breath. She did not understand half the sayings her mother came up with any more than she understood why someone would need to travel all the way to Nepal to think things over. And yet her mother always had a refreshing point of view—in a strange way. "Thanks, mom."

Later, when Kit was lying in bed, she decided her

mother had made a good point. It was wonderful simply to know a fabulous man like Mark Dawson existed. She could admire him from afar, enjoy her work, and try to be happy for him. And Ruby. Yuck. The thought brought a tear down her face. Then another. And another.

Kit reached for the tissue box on the nightstand. Empty. She felt around the foot of the bed for her Kate Spade pocketbook, which was still where she had tossed it earlier. She dug around for a Kleenex and instead came up with a white linen handkerchief with the letter *D* embroidered on one corner in crisp navy thread. *D* as in Dawson. "Keep it in case you need it," Mark had told her in the taxicab. Kit held it against her face and sniffed. It smelled clean and woodsy, like him. She drifted off to sleep, clutching it in one hand.

Chapter Six

Weddings, the Van Winterden Way: An engagement or wedding announcement may be place in local newspapers.

T he Skylight Ballroom of The St. Regis hotel hummed with activity. An army of waiters marched through the room, putting final touches to tables that were set with the hotel's signature Tiffany silver. A team of florists unloaded armloads of fresh-cut flowers from the service elevator. A radio squawked. A cell phone rang.

Kit stifled a yawn. It was barely 7:00 A.M.

She watched a production crew from *Big Breakfast* lay yards of cable for a live video feed of the Happy Couple with the Great White. Today was a big day. Happy Couple was going to announce they had selected The St. Regis to host their wedding.

Ruby marched out of the ladies' room, perfectly

made-up. She scanned the ballroom, and perked up at the sight of the video crew. If she saw Kit, she gave no indication. Which was a good thing.

The producer of *Big Breakfast* scurried over to Ruby, as did The St. Regis P.R. woman. The three chatted as though they were old friends. Ruby was the perfect contestant, just as she was the perfect bride-to-be, re-splendent this morning in a svelte brown pants suit topped with an Hermes scarf.

Kit forced herself to look away, flipped open her lap-top, and pretended to focus on work.

Mark Dawson appeared in the doorway, fresh from his own makeover in the men's room.

He looked, Kit thought, like a movie star. The makeup team had blown out his hair so it looked thicker than ever, and had done something to make his eyes look even deeper and warmer than usual. It proved Edgar's theory that even straight men looked better with makeup.

Mark surveyed the scene before him and let out a long, low whistle. The ballroom, with its cove ceiling and rows of French doors lining two long walls, had been designed in the style of the Hall of Mirrors at Ver-sailles. Many of New York's most elite gatherings had been held here since the hotel's grand opening in 1906. Kit had done her homework.

Mark spotted Kit at her table just inside the entrance and headed her way.

"Mark!" Ruby yelled. "Yoo-hoo, honey! We're over here." She waved frantically, motioning for Mark to join her at the other side of the ballroom. *Now.*

"Be right there," Mark replied, striding purposefully towards Kit.

"How are you holding up?" Mark said, shaking her hand. He held it for perhaps a second or two longer than was necessary. But maybe not. "Everything okay?"

Kit nodded, aware they were being watched. "Fine."

He gave a slight frown.

"I'm here, still standing to tell the tale," she said, attempting to sound breezy. She gave what she hoped was a confident smile. Because she didn't feel very plucky.

"Good," Mark said.

The room's early morning chill seemed to disappear. Kit felt better than she had in days.

"Chin up," he said. He looked as though he wanted to say more, but they were joined by Ruby.

"There you are, Kit, hiding in the corner like a little mouse," Ruby said. "I didn't even know you were here."

Kit felt her cheeks flame as though she had been slapped. But it was, after all, time to face the music. Kit called to mind her mother's advice. Learn what she needed to, do her job, and move on. Kit extended her hand to Ruby. "Good morning."

Ruby accepted her handshake with all the energy of a dead fish. "I wouldn't have thought you needed to be here at all," she said.

"I wouldn't miss it," Kit replied. The truth was, she had been ordered to attend their news announcement by way of a terse email from Mrs. Van Winterden, flagged "Urgent." It was the sort of offer nobody would refuse.

So, Kit had set her alarm clock early and arrived at 6:00, Starbucks in hand, well ahead of the taping set to begin at 7:30. She had reviewed her notes, read the morning paper, and watched the grand old hotel wake up and greet the day. Better to be early than risk running late. Traffic was always heavy near Fifth Avenue, especially at morning rush hour. And Great White was never late. That would violate one of her primary rules of etiquette. So Kit couldn't afford to be late either. Not if she wanted to stay on as associate editor of *White Weddings* magazine.

"Grab us some coffee, will you?" Ruby said. "I take mine black with a Sweet 'n Low on the side."

Kit bit her tongue. She was a reporter, not Ruby's private servant. She was about to inform Ruby of that fact when she heard the unmistakable whispery voice of Great White, who chose that moment to appear soundlessly at Kit's elbow.

Kit practically jumped out of her skin.

"The butler will see to that," Mrs. Van Winterden said, looking regal this morning in a plum suit. "The St. Regis is quite well known for its butlers. Many royals stay here because they can enjoy the comforts of home without the expense of traveling with their household staff."

Ruby turned red. Apparently every bride should know how to boss around a butler.

"Kit will use this time to gather information on the advantages of hosting a wedding at The St. Regis hotel," Mrs. Van Winterden said. She gave a slight nod in Kit's direction.

Kit was thankful her laptop was already open, humming, and ready to go. She would be sure to write an informative article about the attributes of the grand hotel, including its top-notch staff and exquisite marble lobby. For comparison's sake, she would also list event spaces available at other tony hotels such as the Pierre hotel a few blocks up Fifth Avenue, St. Moritz and the super-deluxe Regency Hotel on nearby Park Avenue as well as the Four Seasons on East Fifty-seventh Street.

Great White waved her hand to indicate the couple should sit at a table, then busied herself reviewing sound bites with the hotel PR woman and the producer.

Kit snuck a look at Mark across the table. He was much better looking than the anchorman from *Big Breakfast,* Kit thought. In fact, Mark looked like a movie star of the Brad Pitt variety, all strong jaw and square shoulders.

The thought was enough to make her blush. Darn. Her face was giving her away again. The fact remained, however, that Mark Dawson was the best-looking man she had ever met. And the sweetest. And the absolute nicest. Not to mention the sexiest. There was no question about that. And here he was, sitting across from her at this very table, engaged to marry someone else.

Mark leaned in close from across the table.

Kit held her breath.

"What can we tell you?" he asked with a smile.

Ruby studied her fingernails.

Kit tried to steady herself. She took a breath and told herself to focus. "For starters, how do you feel about holding the reception here?" Kit's voice, when she spoke, came out in a high-pitched squeak. Nerves.

Ruby came briefly to life. "We would have been happy anywhere on Fifth Avenue between Forty-second Street and the upper Sixties." She had neatly mapped out the highest-priced real estate in the world, taking in Rockefeller Plaza, Trump Tower and the eastern boundary of the diamond district for good measure.

"I see," Kit murmured, typing fast.

"We wanted some place really special," Mark added, "and The St. Regis has it all. History, service, atmosphere."

Not to be outdone, Ruby added, "I think it's a grand place for a wedding," she declared. "Simply grand."

Kit tapped away at her keyboard, aware that Ruby was watching her take down every word.

"It is a sad fact, but one attends so many dreadful weddings these days," Ruby said, warming to her subject. "Thank heaven, we are the lucky ones. We are able to avoid that fate—thanks to Mrs. Van Winterden, *White Weddings* magazine and The St. Regis hotel."

She must have been up all night, dreaming up sound bites, Kit thought. This interview was going to be lacking in spontaneity.

Mark spoke up, thankfully. "I think what matters most is simply to enjoy the day, no matter where the wedding takes place. A lot of people forget that their wedding day is also the first day of their marriage."

Kit took it all down under a mental heading marked, "Too Good to be True."

"Both people need to remember the reason for their wedding day. It's a celebration of their decision to join their lives together. But it shouldn't take on a life of its own. So in that sense, it doesn't matter where the wedding is held."

Kit continued typing at her laptop, aware that he continued to watch her with those liquid brown eyes.

Ruby was bent over her Blackberry, busily tapping away at its tiny keyboard.

"The hotel really has nothing to do with it, when you think about it," Mark continued. "The St. Regis is a great hotel. Don't get me wrong."

As if that were possible. Kit smiled at him.

Mark looked around the elegant ballroom. "My parents eloped, and they've been happily married for thirty years. So I guess I've always believed the wedding itself isn't that important."

He was speaking as though he could see what was written in Kit's heart. She had edited one too many articles with titles like, "Ice Sculpture for a White Hot Dessert Table." So his words were music to her ears. She longed to tell him she had sat through four of her parents' collective weddings, and felt the same way he did.

But she didn't, of course. Instead, she gazed at him and imagined she was seeing stars.

Poof! Kit *was* seeing stars. *Poof!* A camera flash popped nearby. A large burly man approached, snapping away, inches from their table.

Ruby lifted her head, now on high alert. "Who are you with?"

"The *Post.* This'll run tomorrow morning," the man said, snapping a few more photos.

"Great," Ruby beamed. "Everyone will see this photo." She pecked Mark on his cheek with excitement.

Kit couldn't be sure, but it appeared to her that Mark winced.

Ruby wiped away the small smudge of lipstick she'd left on Mark's cheek and reached into her bag for her cell phone. "My agent will love this," she said, hitting her speed dial.

Mark gazed at Kit, blinking several times. "I think I've got stars in my eyes."

Kit melted. "Me, too."

"I have a bad feeling," Kit said later. She helped herself to another handful of M & M's from the bowl on Edgar's desk, and popped one into her mouth. It was the end of the workday and the offices were quiet except for a whirring noise as Edgar rewound the videotape from the morning's *Big Breakfast* show.

"Don't be silly," Edgar said. "That segment was perfect. The happy couple made their big announcement. Great White was there, you were there, you got your interview. End of story. Right?"

"I guess," Kit replied. The taping *had* gone perfectly, that much was true. But Kit did not like the way Great White had watched her, practically boring holes into Kit with her tiny black eyes.

"You're overreacting, Cookie," Edgar said firmly.

"Maybe. But I have a bad feeling about this. She's not been happy with me since I had to run out of that church." Kit carefully separated the red M & M's from the others and popped them in her mouth.

Edgar shrugged. "Things are going well. You're doing your part. And Great White's got a million things to think about besides you." He tapped the cassette for emphasis. "The wedding is coming up fast. Great White will have her fifteen minutes of fame, thereby selling loads of books. She laughs all the way to the bank. You get a promotion. And I ride along on your coattails." Edgar placed the videocassette in its plastic sleeve and handed it to Kit. "Put this in your "Kudos' " file, Cookie. Go home and stop worrying. I'll tell you when to worry."

Kit's heart dropped to the floor next morning when she heard Edgar's voice on her answering machine.

"Time to worry. Call me."

Still damp from her shower, she had noticed the blinking light and hit the play button. Nobody ever called this early.

Kit's blood ran cold at the sound of Edgar's voice. It was serious. She hit the speed dial button and called his apartment. No answer. She dialed his office number next.

Edgar picked up on the first ring. "Cookie?"

Kit heard the tension in his voice right away. "What's up?" She wasn't sure she wanted to know.

"Have you seen this morning's *Post?*" Kit got an icy feeling in the pit of her stomach. Bad karma, as her mother would say.

"Not yet," Kit said.

"You'd better pick one up and get in here fast," Edgar said. "Sorry, Cookie, it's not good."

The icy feeling quickly became a solid block of ice.

"The gossip page has a big spread on the happy couple in The St. Regis hotel," Edgar said.

"What's wrong with that?" Kit asked, her knees turning spongy.

"There's a big close-up photo of Mark being swooned all over," Edgar said.

"So?" Kit remembered the photographer who had shown up at their table.

"The headline reads, *'She Only Has Eyes for Him.'* "

Kit felt faint. "Go on." But she thought she had a pretty good idea of what the problem might be.

"The woman in the photo is you," Edgar said.

Kit hung up the phone and dressed, with shaking hands, in her most conservative navy suit.

She stopped at the corner newsstand and bought two copies of the *Post*, then hailed a cab instead of taking the crosstown bus as she normally would.

She settled into the back seat, opened *The Post* to "Page Six" with a silent prayer that the article wouldn't be as bad as Edgar had made it out to be.

It was worse. As if the photo and headline weren't bad enough, the copy was deliciously gossipy, the sort Kit usually liked to read:

The Big Apple's most famous bride-to-be has stars in her eyes, and who can blame her? We hear the reception will be held at the posh St. Regis Hotel, where hot and cold running butlers are part of the package. Bring your own groom, though. This one (Mark Dawson, pictured) is happily spoken for, by the looks of things.

Kit felt her stomach lurch. She studied the photo more carefully. It was a good one, probably the best ever taken of her. She looked radiant. In love. Kit groaned aloud.

The cab came to a stop in front of the steel and glass office tower on Sixth Avenue that housed *White Weddings* and several sister publications. It was where she worked—at least for today.

Kit paid the cabbie and raced inside, stopping at Security before squeezing onto a crowded express elevator.

As the car began its ascent, someone reached from behind and pressed something into her hand. It was a rolled up copy of today's *Post*.

Kit felt her face flush the color of a hothouse tomato.

"Congratulations, Kit!" said a female voice that belonged to one of the copy editors.

"Nice photo!" called someone else. Kit heard a chorus of snickers. She was grateful when the elevator stopped at her floor.

The door opened and she made her escape, practically mowing down Mrs. Van Winterden.

Great White stood stock still, turning her spectacles fully on Kit. Other staffers scattered, leaving Kit alone and feeling like a hunted baby seal.

Mrs. Van Winterden looked Kit over as though she had turned up unexpectedly in a fisherman's net.

Kit was glad she had worn her best interview suit though at the moment she wasn't sure it would do her any good.

"Come to my office in fifteen minutes." Great White said in her usual low, throaty voice. "Bring your notes." Without waiting for a reply, she turned and jabbed the elevator *Up* button with one tiny finger. The doors opened at once as though even the elevator did not dare keep the founding editor waiting.

Kit watched the doors slide shut, wondering if she should clean out her desk. She made a beeline for Edgar's office. The door was shut. She rapped once, then barged in.

Frowning, Edgar looked up from his light board. When he saw Kit, he ran around his desk and gave her a hug.

"Cookie." He pursed his lips in sympathy. "Have you met with her yet?"

"Not yet," Kit said, shaking her head.

"She was down here looking for you first thing this morning," Edgar said.

"I guess she reads the *Post*," Kit said. "I have a meeting with her in five minutes. She told me to bring my notes."

Edgar's eyes widened in alarm but he said, "It'll be okay."

His face, however, told Kit he was only trying to cheer her up.

"Whatever you do, don't cry." he tried to look encouraging. "You'll ruin your mascara."

Kit fought back tears. "Right," she said, taking a tissue from the box he pushed across the desk. She sat down heavily on one of the chairs. He was right, of course. She should try to bow out with dignity. After all, she was about to be chewed out by the woman at the helm of the one of the most profitable magazines in the world, catering to the vast fifty-five-billion-dollar wedding industry. That was something.

"Stupid paparazzi," Edgar said.

Kit felt more tears well up, hot and stinging. She knew the mistaken identity in the *Post* wasn't the problem. The real problem was the way she looked in the photo—like a woman in love.

The last thing on her mind when she was awarded this assignment was the possibility that it might hurt her career. But that is exactly what seemed to be happening. The thought tightened the knot in her stomach. She grimaced in pain.

Edgar clucked sympathetically. "I wish there was something I could do."

Kit absently smoothed her skirt, wishing he could, too. But there was no escape.

A short while later she found herself perched on the edge of her chair at Mrs. Van Winterden's large mahogany Queen Anne desk.

There was a spectacular view from the wall of windows behind the desk facing north toward Central Park. One corner of the massive suite held a butler's pantry, complete with a brass Italian espresso maker and a dainty set of demitasse cups and matching saucers. Mrs. Van Winterden did not offer any refreshment, however.

Kit's chair was several inches closer to the ground than Mrs. Van Winterden's Aeron chair, which had the effect of making Kit feel small. It was probably deliberate.

Mrs. Van Winterden was on a call when Kit entered, murmuring some sort of apology in a soothing tone. She promised the caller she would take steps to remedy the situation immediately. Today. Kit felt hackles rise on the back of her neck.

Mrs. Van Winterden replaced the receiver and

swiveled to face Kit. Bright sunshine spilled into the room from the windows behind her desk, making it difficult to see the eyes behind her tortoise spectacles.

Kit squinted up at her.

"Ms. McCabe, I am having serious doubt that you are ready to take on a cover assignment for a national magazine," Mrs. Van Winterden said.

Kit thought that what she'd heard about the magazine's founding editor was true. She was not the one to mince words. Kit nodded miserably.

Great White stared at her. "You had to leave Mid-Manhattan Church the other day due to health issues, which caused some anxiety to Ms. Lattingly and Mr. Dawson. Of course we all suffer from health issues from time to time. That's understandable."

Except it wasn't. Kit nodded.

Mrs. Van Winterden continued, "And there has been some confusion surrounding this assignment." She glanced at a corner of her desk, to a copy of today's *Post*. "Of course that's not your fault."

Except it was, Kit thought miserably.

"I think it's time to evaluate whether this assignment is working out."

There it was. To her horror, Kit felt the corners of her mouth yank downward. She blinked back tears. She tried to swallow but found her throat blocked by a large, hot lump. She pressed her fingers to her lips and tapped them gently, trying to stop the sobs that were fighting to come out, buying time until she could speak. She had waited years to win this assignment, and was not about to give it up without a fight.

Great White made a tiny steeple with her fingers, waiting. "Frankly, Ms. McCabe, I think it's time we reassign this story to another, more seasoned editor."

More seasoned. The words stung. Kit's big chance was slipping away before her eyes. "I think I can turn things around," she said.

Great White arched an eyebrow.

"I realize we've hit a bump," Kit said, careful not to sound like she was pleading—though she was. "But I feel I've built up a certain rapport with our contest-winning couple." *Hah. Well, half of the couple anyway.* "I've gathered a lot of background notes, and a lot of insights that will give depth to my story. I think we'll sacrifice that by bringing someone else on board at this point. And I don't foresee any more mishaps." Kit waited, miserable, hardly daring to breathe.

Mrs. Van Winterden settled back in her aerodynamically-designed chair, removed her glasses, and massaged a red spot on the bridge of her nose. Minus the trademark lenses, Great White's eyes looked larger but unfocused. Kit remembered having read somewhere that sharks have poor vision. They rely on a keen sense of smell to hunt their prey.

"We have, as you pointed out, invested a lot of time in this," Great White finally said. "Bringing on someone new at this point would pose further difficulties for the magazine as well as for our winning couple." She turned her black eyes directly on Kit.

Kit tried not to squirm.

"And so for now, I'll keep you on this story. But let's be very clear, Ms. McCabe. I don't want any further mishaps. If you have any problems with this assignment, you need to discuss them with me before they get out of hand. Understood?"

A flood of relief washed over Kit, but she tried not to show it. She was afraid it might antagonize Great White. She nodded meekly instead. "Thank you. I'll do my very best."

Great White stared at her for another long moment. "We can't ask for more than that, can we?"

Kit shuddered. She thanked Mrs. Van Winterden once more and rose to go. The interview was over. She was halfway to the door when the sound of that whispery voice stopped her in her tracks once more.

"One more thing," the founding editor called after her. "Please take whatever medication is necessary to get your allergies under control by Friday night. I need to have you on your toes for the Lattingly's engagement party."

"Pop a Benadryl and you'll be fine." Edgar expertly scooped up a piece of yellowtail sushi with his chopsticks.

"That's what Great White said," Kit said glumly.

Edgar chuckled. "Tell me again. She said not to do anything to increase the anxiety level? We work at a monthly bridal magazine, for heaven's sake. How much less anxiety could someone have and still be in publishing?"

Kit sighed. "I have no idea. At this point, just my presence seems to make everything worse." She checked the restaurant to see if anybody from work was within earshot before continuing. The coast was clear.

They were dining at their favorite Japanese place, on Second Avenue in the East Fifties, far from the office. The only person within range was the sushi chef, who was busy hacking away at a piece of flash-frozen mackerel and probably spoke no English anyway.

"Hiring a stripper would liven things up," Edgar said sarcastically as he selected another Inside-out eelskin roll and swirled it through his soy dish before popping it into his mouth. He finished chewing and took a sip of sake. "And take the heat off you."

Kit looked at him sharply. She thought back to the countless sakes they had shared here, toasting their future with small ceramic cups. Now Kit had finally landed the cover story they'd both hoped and planned for. It was her big chance. But here they were, weighing the odds of her managing to see the big assignment through to the end. "What do you mean?"

"I mean you wouldn't have to focus on Mark and Ruby as much." Edgar put his cup down and looked at her. He was suddenly serious. "Let me ask you something. And don't get upset, okay?"

Kit frowned.

"What is it with you and this guy?"

Kit said nothing, but hurt feelings made color rise in her cheeks. She leaned back in her chair slowly before answering. "Nothing," she said finally.

Edgar pursed his lips. "Really? You've been talking about him since you met him. And honestly, Cookie, the look on your face in the *Post* does say it all."

That was the last straw. Kit put her chopsticks down abruptly. "That photo was a mistake. It had nothing to do with me."

"I know that, Cookie." Edgar held one hand up. "I'm just saying I've never seen that look on your face before."

"Well, so what?" Kit knew she sounded defensive.

"It's just that you look . . . well . . . happy." Edgar smiled.

Kit swallowed. She wondered who had come up with the idea to wrap raw fish in seaweed and eat it, anyway. "Well, he is a nice man." It sounded lame and she knew it. She stared at the remains of her sushi platter and waited for Edgar to say something. He said nothing for a long while, reminding her that he was a wise man indeed. After some time passed she snuck a look at him.

He was beaming at her. "C'mon, Cookie. Get real. There's nothing wrong with having a crush on someone."

A crush? Kit searched for the right words. This was not a crush. Mark Dawson had rocked her world. She hadn't been able to stop thinking of him since the day they'd met. The way he smiled. The sound of his voice, which was like a warm bath. The way he looked at her. The way he spoke to her. The way he seemed to understand her thoughts. The strength in his hands. The way he'd looked at her standing at that altar, his voice low and sweet and reaching inside her, all the way to her heart . . .

"Uh-oh. It's worse than I thought." The smile faded from Edgar's face.

"What?" Kit felt her cheeks flush. "Stop."

"It's more than a crush, I see. Say no more. I can read it on your face." Edgar tended toward melodrama but he was a good friend to have, especially at times like this.

"I wasn't expecting it," Kit said finally. "To feel like

this." She didn't dare name it, even to herself. All she knew was that she'd never felt this way before about any of the men she'd dated since college. Ever since meeting Mark Dawson, she had felt like she was walking on a cushion of air, ten feet above the ground. "It's silly, I know."

"Don't say that!" Edgar protested. "There's nothing silly about being in love."

There. Someone had said it. Finally. The word had been rumbling around in her brain, down deep. Not daring to rise to the surface. She'd never before said it, or even thought it, in relation to herself. In fact, she'd begun to wonder if she was even capable of it. But Mark Dawson had hit her like a ton of bricks, and she knew instinctively that what she was feeling was the stuff of all the song lyrics and magazine articles. "It's not that," Kit protested weakly.

Edgar gave a triumphant wave of his hand. "I knew it. You've been glowing. I've seen it in your face for days."

And now, so had everyone else in New York City. At least everyone who read the *Post*. One picture had shifted her career solidly onto a downhill track—steep and fast—despite the fact that Mark Dawson was about to marry someone else.

"What are you going to do?" Edgar frowned.

Kit shrugged, "Nothing."

Edgar sat forward, surprised. "Nothing? Listen, Cookie, there aren't very many wonderful men around. And Mark Dawson is a keeper. He's smart, funny, kind, handsome. And he's not afraid to spend on a ring, according to that *Post* column."

Kit flinched. As everyone knew, the *Post* always got the story right.

"And he's a natty dresser. I like a man who can pull off a double-breasted suit. But in the end none of that matters," he continued. "All that really matters is that you are in love with him. Some people live their whole lives without meeting their mates. Maybe you've met yours. You can't just ignore it."

Sometimes Edgar *was* more than skin-deep, reminding Kit why she treasured him so. "I'm not ignoring it," Kit said stubbornly. "I'm just facing facts. He's getting married in just a few days' time. That is the only reason I even met him. This time next week, I'll be on deadline to turn in my story about his wedding. And the week after that, he'll be history."

"But, Cookie," Edgar protested, "you've met him now for a reason. He's not married. Not yet. Not at this moment."

"He almost is."

"Almost ain't the same as a done deal," Edgar said with conviction.

It was the first time they had ever disagreed on anything major. Not a good sign.

"If I was meant to be with him, I'd have met him before he was engaged," Kit said wearily.

Edgar harrumphed. "Listen, Cookie. I never believed in all that karma stuff your mother talks about—at least not until now. But this guy seems like the real thing. He came into your life for a reason. And you've fallen for him. You can't just ignore that. You've got high morals. Everyone who knows you can vouch for that. You could have married for convenience long ago. But this is the real deal, and all's fair in love and war. You can't pull a Joan-of-Arc on me now."

"Yes, I can," Kit replied. "I need to do my job, forget all about him and treat him the same way he's treating me. Namely, as a nice person he met by chance. That's it. End of story."

Edgar looked unconvinced. "How do you know you're not acting out of fear? Fighting your own karma?"

So, all those times Edgar had looked bored he had actually been listening, soaking up pearls of wisdom from Mother's Lama. Because now he was spouting it back at her.

"How do you know it's not your fear of commitment getting in the way of your happiness?" Edgar asked quietly.

Ouch. Looking back, Kit would remember this as the day Edgar started to believe in karma.

Mark Dawson's day had gotten off to a fairly good start. He had slid out of bed at six, showered, and toweled dry. He had just lathered up to shave when he heard it—an ear-splitting scream. It was coming from the tiny living room of his one-bedroom apartment.

The hair on the back of his neck stood on end as he threw open the bathroom door and raced through the bedroom. He knew that voice.

"Ruby!" he yelled. Every muscle in his body was flexed and ready for a fight. There was a baseball bat in the hall closet he could swing at an intruder if need be, even though he had no idea how an intruder could have followed Ruby past the doorman and up to his apartment. But he was ready to protect Ruby with his life if necessary. Mark sprinted to the living room and found her, giving him an accusing stare from inside her floor-length mahogany mink coat with the starburst pattern of female pelts. She appeared unharmed. Relief flooded through him.

"Are you okay?" Mark said, bounding across the room. "What's going on?"

She shook her head wordlessly and held out a copy of the *New York Post.* "I got up early," she said.

Ruby was not an early riser. And she wasn't due at The Haberdashery until 9:30. Which meant he'd never seen her at this hour of the morning. Mark rubbed his jaw thoughtfully.

She thrust the newspaper in his direction. "I wanted to surprise you before you left for work. We're supposed to be in there today and . . . and . . . ," her voice trailed off sadly. She shook her head.

Mark remembered the events of the day before, including the photographer who had shown up at The St. Regis hotel. Their photo would run in this morning's *Post,* he had told them. Apparently, it had.

Mark looked at Ruby quizzically. "Bad photo?" Ruby was fussy about how she looked on camera.

"Read it!" Ruby thrust the paper at him.

There in the "*Page Six*" gossip column was a photo of Mark with Kit McCabe, looking as though *they* were the toast of the town. Complete with a big head-line and a story. Mark studied the page for a few sec-

onds. It was, he thought, a pretty good photo. Kit Mc-
Cabe was a beautiful woman. Not in a flashy, super-
model sort of way. More of a classic beauty, he
decided. Inside and out. And there she was, in black
and white, smiling up at him. He swelled with pride.
No doubt about it, Kit McCabe had a thing for him.
There was the proof, clear as day. They looked good
together.

"Mark!" Ruby shot him a look of pure disgust. "Just
look at that photo! Aren't you upset?"

Not really, Mark thought. "Honey, please," he began. "It's a simple case of mistaken identity. No big
deal." A mistake had been made. But the mistake was
not his. This meant he was not in hot water with Ruby,
which had been the case with increasing frequency
lately. But not this time. Relief flooded through him.
He chuckled.

Ruby stared at him, aghast. "This is not funny!"

"It's no big deal," he said. "You can't tell me you're
upset about this." Too late, he realized she was.

"Upset?" Ruby shrieked. "I told my agent I'd be in
the paper today. He told his contacts on cable to watch
for me. We're talking about an option for a reality TV
show. Everyone I know will be looking at this." Her
voice broke.

Mark hated it when Ruby cried. Lately, with this
blasted contest and wedding, it seemed to be a daily
event. He took a deep breath. "Sweet Pea, please," he
began.

Ruby stamped her foot. "Just look at this photo! That
woman is out to ruin our wedding!"

That woman, meaning Kit. It was unfair, Mark thought. The photo was a mistake on the part of the photo editor at the *Post.* It was not Kit's fault.

"Just look at her," Ruby waved the paper aloft. "Like *she's* the one getting married instead of me!" Ruby stamped her foot.

Mark bit back a sigh. He hated it when Ruby got like this. When they first started dating, everything was so simple. Ruby was beautiful, and he felt proud walking into a restaurant or party with a tall blond on his arm. After they'd been dating a while, she'd begun dropping hints about where the relationship was going. It was okay with Mark, because he figured they might eventually get married. Eventually. Just not right away. And then along came that stupid contest, and it moved everything into fast forward bringing out the worst qualities in Ruby. Mark gulped. He was not in the mood for this. It was just plain too early in the morning, for one thing. "Sweetie, look," Mark began.

"No," Ruby shot back. "You look! You're taking her side in this! And I won't tolerate it!" Ruby stamped her foot again. Two bright spots of color appeared high on her cheeks.

Bad sign. Mark had seen Ruby's tantrums before, more times than he cared to count. And he didn't want to see her turn her anger on Kit McCabe. None of this was Kit's fault. She was just trying to do her job. He remembered the day he had met her in the taxicab on the way to The Plaza Hotel, and how nervous she was. But she'd handled it well. He saw in his mind's eye the way her silk blouse had clung to her when it was damp, revealing the full curves of her body. Not to mention her full red lips. And the way her hair kept spilling forward no matter how much she tried to smooth it back. Very sexy. Not to mention her easy laugh and great sense of humor.

He snuck another glance at the photo in the paper. Yup. She was a real looker. And she had the hots for him. A small, proud smile came to Mark's lips in spite of himself.

"Mark!" Ruby shrieked again. Eyes widening, she shook her head in disbelief.

Mark took a deep swallow as the smile faded from his face. "Listen, Ruby," he began, trying not to sound defensive. But it was too late. He knew Ruby saw, plain as day on his face, the fact that Mark was powerless to stop the feelings he had for Kit. Just thinking of Kit McCabe was enough to distract him from all thoughts related to planning his wedding. Mark gulped again, grateful Ruby couldn't read his mind as well as she could read the expression on his face, which even a thick layer of shaving cream couldn't hide.

"Honey, please, let's laugh about this," he began, moving toward her.

She gave him a look that stopped him in his tracks. "You might think she's harmless, but I don't," Ruby said. "I've had just about enough of Kit McCabe!" She turned on her heel and left, slamming the door behind her.

All morning an email snaked its way through the editorial offices of the *New York Post* and its main rival, the *New York Daily News*. Mistakes in either newsroom were pounced on with glee by reporters at both papers. There was even a Blooper Hall of Fame. And so the photo misidentifying Kit as Mark's intended bride made the rounds quickly. Adding to the hilarity was the fact that Kit McCabe was a journalist herself.

Things did not improve for Mark as the morning wore on. After Ruby left he dressed for work and headed out, only to step into a tangle of leashes and tiny dogs when he got outside. Mark skipped from one foot to the other as the dogs snarled, baring tiny teeth at him.

A tiny old woman in a big mink coat tugged on their leashes and tried to shush them. As she apologized to Mark over the din, a wave of recognition washed over her face. "I know you. I saw your picture in the paper today. You won that wedding."

One of the dogs sniffed Mark's pant leg. He stepped back, out of harm's way, and nodded.

The lady wagged a finger at him, smiling. "Listen to me, young man. I want to tell you something."

Mark glanced at his watch. This was his fifteen minutes of fame.

"There is no greater gift than true love. I had it with my husband, and I was married for fifty-three years." The woman took a step closer.

Mark kept an eye on the yapping dogs.

"You have it," she said, wagging a finger. "I could tell by that picture, the way your girlfriend looks at you."

Kit. She meant Kit. A buzz of pure pleasure tickled him at the base of his spine and moved up. Mark gave a real smile for the first time that day.

The lady yanked on the leashes and turned to go. "Don't take it for granted, young man. A lot of people go through life without ever knowing true love."

Mark took a step in the opposite direction. "Have a nice day."

"Trust me," the woman called over her shoulder. "The camera doesn't lie. I can see it in your eyes. And your children will be blessed with a sweet disposition. Just like her."

Her words were with him when he arrived at work. He stepped aboard an express elevator and watched the floor numbers flash on the electronic display as the car rose high above Wall Street. He heard giggling behind him.

One of the interns held a copy of the *Post*.

Mark felt the muscles in his jaw contract.

"Congratulations. You're a cute couple." The intern smiled at him. "And you won a free wedding. That's so exciting."

It was, after all, every bride's dream. Mark gave a tight smile. "Thanks."

There was another copy of the *Post* waiting on his desk. Someone had drawn pointy horns and a goatee on Mark, with a message scrawled on top: "Congratulations! Who will it be?"

Good question. Mark sat in his chair, tipping it all the way back until he faced the ceiling. His father had warned him there were times in every marriage when a man felt an interest in another woman. But what if it happened *before* the wedding? Mark scowled and let his chair down with a thump. He hated indecision. He took one last look at the *Post* before tossing it in the trash. He looked up the number of a florist, dialed it, and placed two large orders. One for Ruby and another for Ruby's mother. That should get things back on track.

Women loved flowers.

Chapter Seven

*Weddings, the Van Winterden Way: An engagement
party is the couple's first official appearance together.
It is a joyous occasion!*

Kit stared at her computer screen and frowned. It
was no use trying to work. Each time she tried to focus,
Mark's face swam before her eyes. She was due at his
engagement party in a few short hours, and had spent
much of Friday afternoon working on her cover story
about his wedding.

She had read through Ruby's winning contest entry
so many times the lines had blurred before her eyes.
There was no mistaking why the judges had chosen it,
Kit thought grimly.

"I dreamed of the perfect wedding since I was a little
girl, dressing my dolls in bits of white organza and
tulle, giving them receptions in the backyard," Ruby
had written.

Touching, Kit had thought, even though the back-yard was a waterfront estate on Long Island's famed Gold Coast, and the dolls had most likely been dressed to Ruby's specifications by the Lattingly's live-in help.

"And one day, my Prince Charming finally arrived to sweep me off my feet," the entry continued.

Fresh from the wilds of Grosse Pointe, Michigan, Kit thought dryly. The town was the Midwest's answer to Beverly Hills.

"I knew then," Ruby's entry continued, "that we needed a ceremony that would show the world we were meant for each other." A ceremony, Kit thought, that would require an entire cargo pallet of fresh-cut gardenias flown in from Costa Rica, several hundred white candles made from bees raised free from pesticides, and all the planning and precision of a major military maneuver.

Kit sighed, and hit the auto-save button. She would have to get a grip on her feelings if she was going to write the best cover story in the history of *White Weddings*.

Approaching footsteps broke the office stillness. The only other sound was the hum of the water cooler. Though it was just after 5:00 P.M., it was early in the monthly life cycle of the magazine. Most of the editors cleared out early during the first two weeks of every month, to make up for the late nights on deadline at the end.

"Incoming!" Edgar's voice rang out, as a chocolate bar sailed over the cubicle wall and landed on Kit's desk.

Kit swiveled away from her screen, grabbed the candy bar and opened the wrapper.

"How's the next editor-in-chief?" Edgar, backpack in tow, moved a pile of unopened mail from a chair and settled in. "Killing time till the big bash, I see."

Kit nodded. She broke the candy bar in two, handing half to Edgar. "I can't face tonight on an empty stomach," she confessed, taking a bite.

Edgar bit into his half and chuckled. "I don't blame you. The dreaded engagement party."

Engagement parties were the official kickoff of every couple's betrothal. The party itself was, according to Mrs. Van Winterden's book, *a fun-filled, light-hearted celebration to usher in the rising tide of well-wishers and flurry of activity that is sure to surround the approach of the big day*. In reality, it was usually a torturous evening spent on one's feet, with a guaranteed hangover the next day.

The party would give Ruby the chance to show off her engagement ring. All four carats? Had he really traded away his grandmother's ring for it? Kit imagined a sweet old lady baking gingerbread cookies, a tasteful round one-carat diamond set in hand-carved platinum on her gnarled fourth finger. Mark must have been heartbroken when Ruby rejected it. The pear-shaped monstrosity from Tiffany must have been Ruby's idea. Kit bit into her candy bar and chewed savagely.

Edgar gave an approving nod at the sight of the black cocktail dress that hung, encased in clear plastic, on the cubicle wall. "The Marc Jacobs, I see. Excellent choice."

They'd spotted the dress together at an end-of-season sale at Bergdorf's last year.

"You'll be dressed to kill," Edgar declared.

Kit frowned.

"But still professional," he added.

"You don't think it's over the top?"

"What shoes?"

"My snakeskin sling-backs."

Edgar smiled. "You'll be fine."

"Good, and that brown lip gloss from Barney's."

"Perfect," Edgar said. "You'll be the belle of the ball. Even the bride will be jealous."

Kit held up a hand in protest. "That's not what I'm after."

"Don't be such a worrywart," Edgar said soothingly. "You'd be a knockout even if you wore a paper bag on your head. Just go and do your job. Nobody's going to think you're out to steal the groom."

His words stayed with her that night.

Kit stood outside the entrance to Mr. and Mrs. Barnard Lattingly's Fifth Avenue penthouse and checked her reflection in the glass. The dress was well worth the paycheck she'd blown, giving a good shape and clean lines while still trim and professional. She had pulled her red hair off her face with a real tortoise-shell clip Edgar had bought her at Harrod's on his trip home last Christmas. Her makeup accentuated her green eyes and strong complexion. For good measure, she had placed tiny dabs of 22 Rue St. Honore, a new scent from Hermes, at strategic pulse points.

The camera around her neck didn't do much to accessorize the outfit, but it gave her the freedom to roam at will.

Kit pressed the buzzer.

A butler ushered her inside a giant foyer with gleaming marble floors, raffia-papered walls, and a gargantuan Murano chandelier. It was like walking into a bank vault.

An army of attendants stood at the ready, bearing silver trays with crystal flutes filled with champagne, orange juice or sparkling water. Another Van Winterden rule: *Always offer a healthy choice for those guests who might be on a low-carb diet or fresh out of rehab.* Kit declined any refreshment in order to keep her hands free for greetings and photos. Mrs. Van Winterden would approve.

A large archway led to a cavernous living room where, just inside, the happy couple waited to greet the horde of well-wishing guests.

"Kit, glad to see you."

Mark's eyes flicked up and down the dress, and Kit sent a silent thanks to the house of Marc Jacobs. He looked like he had stepped straight out of the pages of *People* magazine's *Most Beautiful People* issue. He was handsome as ever in a navy suit and gold silk tie. Not to mention those eyes again, twinkling like lights on a Christmas tree.

Mark held out his hand. Strong and warm, and his grasp caused a fluttering inside her, like doves taking flight. Kit was glad she had come.

A familiar voice put an end to the fluttering, and called to mind the frozen food section at the supermarket. "Look at you, all dressed up. They must have given you the day off." Ruby draped an arm through Mark's so the other hand rested on top. It wasn't the left hand. The one with the ring attached to the third finger. That ring was hard to miss, even when it was resting on Mark's arm. "Here's Mother and Daddy." Ruby waved her left arm in a broad arc through the air.

She must have practiced in the mirror all week, Kit thought sourly.

A very tanned couple appeared. The woman wore a tiny black dress—probably Armani judging by the tapered lapels on the plunging neckline—topped with gold chains and chunky topaz earrings. Her husband was thin on top and thick in the middle. Mr. and Mrs. Barnard Lattingly of Great Neck, Long Island. Ruby's parents.

Mr. Lattingly shook Kit's hand.

Mrs. Lattingly did not. When she spoke, her voice was low and tight, her words measured.

Like someone who had been planning what to say.

"We've heard all about you."

All about you. As though Kit's likeness was hanging on the wall of every post office in America. Kit inched back, her mouth turning dry. She took a breath and braced herself. Might as well get it over with. "I do apologize for that photo in the *New York Post* . . ."

Ruby erupted with movement, her free arm waving wildly. Her voice was loud and high-pitched. "Come, darling, there's someone important." She yanked Mark's arm hard.

The hair on the back of Kit's neck stiffened.

"Excuse us," Mark said.

But Ruby already had her back to them. Mark followed, leaving Kit alone in enemy territory. She swallowed and tried again. "Of course, *White Weddings* had nothing to do with the mix-up."

"Don't speak of it." Mrs. Lattingly made a slicing motion in the air.

The words would sound good on paper, Kit thought, but they didn't match the tone of the woman's voice or the tightness around her mouth.

Mr. Lattingly studied the tops of his shoes.

His wife's next words sent a sharp pang of fear through Kit. "My daughter and I have discussed it with your boss."

The words hung in the air like a cloud of thirsty mosquitoes. Kit couldn't think of anything to say that might help, so she said nothing. She glanced idly at a huge arrangement of cut flowers on a nearby table. It looked like it belonged in a funeral parlor. Finally, Kit remembered to play her trump card. "May I take your photo?"

Mrs. Lattingly brightened. Mr. Lattingly raised his head.

"For my article," Kit explained. She snapped three photos in a row when one might have done. She wanted the effect of the flash more than anything. It worked like it always did.

Ruby came over, Mark in tow.

"May I get a photo of the four of you for my article?" Kit said, knowing what the answer would be.

"Of course you can." Ruby took up a position between her parents and Mark, and flashed Kit a smile meant to dazzle.

It was like watching global warming in action. Kit snapped off a few more, and even asked them to move so she could include the crystal chandelier in the background.

Mrs. Lattingly brightened up. All was forgiven. Kit

was beginning to breathe more easily when Ruby saw more friends arrive. With another wave, she spirited Mark away leaving Kit alone with the Lattinglys again.

Kit noted a flicker across Mrs. Lattingly's face, just before she opened her mouth to speak the words every journalist dreads, "I've got an idea for a cute article."

Kit was not fooled by the woman's bright smile. Mrs. Lattingly was about to make Kit's life a living nightmare.

"Your company also publishes that decorating magazine, right?" Mrs. Lattingly's tone was airy.

The Feathered Nest was the most prestigious publication in its field. The magazines were managed separately, to avoid any conflict of interest though Edgar Lacey had recently been promoted as artistic director for both.

"We're crazy about our designer. You can see the work he's done here." Mrs. Lattingly made a sweeping motion of the giant living room with its beige walls, beige rugs, and beige furniture.

Kit wondered if their decorator also did dentists' waiting rooms.

"He renovated our condo in Miami, too. It's magic. Perfect for *The Feathered Nest.*"

A puff piece. She wanted Kit to write great things about the Miami condo to make up for the mistaken identity in the *Post.* It was an insult even to suggest such a thing. Any editor with a conscience would turn and run. But Kit was in dire straits with this assignment, and she knew it. "Good idea. I'll go in Monday and see what I can do."

Mrs. Lattingly wasn't buying it. "You need to get

some shots of our tumbled stone to really get the feel for the project. Why don't you bring your camera onto the terrace and have a look around?"

Mr. Lattingly turned to his wife. "I don't think she should do that. The terrace is practically a construction zone. There are no lights out there. And she's not dressed for it." He gave Kit a complete once over, top to bottom, to review.

That decided it for his wife. "Nonsense," she snapped. "I'll get the key."

Kit put on her best game face. "Fine." But the Lattinglys were already gone.

She fingered the lens on the camera for a moment, calculating how many shots of the tumbling rocks, or whatever she would need.

Mark walked over. "How are you managing?"

"Fine." Lie.

Mark grinned. "Ruby needed some time with her agent. I'm supposed to be entertaining her sorority sisters." He glanced guiltily over his shoulder. "But I figured I'd see if you needed any help."

The concern in his eyes was genuine. He probably knew his future in-laws pretty well already. Kit ignored the dagger looks she was getting from Ruby's sorority sisters across the room, figuring they'd leave her alone with the groom for only a New York minute. "Thanks," she smiled. She took in a deep gulp of air and realized she'd been holding her breath.

Mark took a sip of his wine. His jaw looked tighter than usual. Kit decided he was as tense as she was. They stood in silence for a moment, like a pair of convicts on a smoking break. Kit was surprised she did not feel the need to speak to fill the silence. She was grateful just to stand next to someone simpatico.

Mark took another sip of his wine. "So, weddings are your specialty?"

Kit giggled. "You could say that." She took a lot of ribbing when she told people she wrote for the world's leading bridal magazine. So she knew before he spoke what his next question would be.

"Got any advice?"

Run for your life. "I've never been married, so I couldn't say."

He raised his eyebrows and shook his head, as if to say it was the craziest thing he had ever heard.

Again Kit couldn't take her eyes off him. At this range she could see the line of his chiseled jaw, and the big dimple in the center of his chin. His cheekbones could have been carved in stone. She was having cocktails with the Marlboro man minus the horse. Kit let out a happy sigh.

Mark parted his lips and prepared to speak.

Kit thought there was a strong possibility she might melt into a puddle right there on the Persian rug.

Mark leaned over her.

Kit swayed a tiny bit.

He frowned. "You, um, have something stuck to your shoulder."

Kit was so focused on him that it took a few seconds for the meaning of his words to sink in. "Huh?"

"Don't look now, but you have a dry cleaning tag stuck to your dress."

Kit felt her cheeks turn beet red.

"Don't panic. I can help." His eyes were twinkling

again. He handed his drink to her and reached around her with one hand.

She felt him graze the back of her bare neck. Something like a musical note trilled down her spine.

"It's stuck. Oh, there's a staple." He reached around with his other hand.

His arms were around her. Kit's insides thrilled to an orchestra only she could hear.

"Almost."

She felt his breath on her bare skin.

"Hold still."

"No problem." He was tall but not overly so. A perfect fit. If she moved her cheek just the tiniest bit they would be touching. The thought made her knees go weak.

"Almost," Mark said.

Almost, indeed.

"Got it." He held up a tiny purple flag to show her.

She knew she should be embarrassed, but he looked positively proud. She couldn't help herself. She giggled.

Mark grinned.

A small cough, too close for comfort, put a stop to the merriment.

Mrs. Ethel Van Winterden had again appeared soundlessly, out of nowhere. She fixed her spectacles on Kit. They were two half moons of reflected light as bright as spotlights in a POW camp.

"Good evening."

Kit was grateful that at least she no longer looked like Minnie Pearl. "Good evening, Mrs. Van Winterden."

Ruby swept up. "Excuse me, but I need my man back. If you don't mind." She locked her arm through Mark's and dragged him away.

Mark excused himself, this time leaving Kit alone with the Great White.

"Enjoying the party?" Mrs. Van Winterden's gaze lingered on the glass in Kit's right hand.

Mark had forgotten his wine glass.

Great White's tiny nose wrinkled.

Drinking on the job. A definite no-no. "It is quite an affair," Kit said. Poor choice of words. She winced.

The top of Mrs. Van Winterden's perfectly coiffed head barely reached Kit's chin, which required Kit to hunch over in order to hear what the older woman had to say. It made Kit feel tall and clumsy.

"I do hope you're getting some photos for the magazine."

"Absolutely. In fact, Mrs. Lattingly has requested some specific shots."

Mrs. Van Winterden reached over and removed the wine glass from Kit's hand. "Good. You need to build a good relationship with our clients, Ms. McCabe."

"Right. I think she needs me right now." Kit spied Ruby's mother across the big room, excusing herself with an awkward motion halfway between a bow and a curtsy.

"There you are," Mrs. Lattingly said as Kit approached. "Follow me. I think you'll get the general idea of what our decorator was trying to accomplish. You can get some pictures to show *The Feathered Nest.* I'm certain that whoever is in charge there will appreciate the fine quality of this work."

Kit's heart sank. The man in charge was none other than Edgar Lacey, art director extraordinaire. "I'll deliver them first thing Monday morning." On her hands and knees, pleading for mercy.

"Follow me." Mrs. Lattingly led the way across the room.

Ruby saw them and fell into step. "Where are you headed, Mother?"

Never one to miss a photo op, Kit thought.

"Just out to the terrace to show our friend around."

"Good idea," Ruby said. "The Park will make a perfect backdrop. I'll join you."

Kit hoped there was a sturdy railing. She was relieved when Mark fell into step behind them. They left the party behind and headed down a dark, narrow hallway that ran the length of the building. It looked like a good place for a mugging.

They reached a tiny room with scuffed walls and a dim flourescent light. A steel door with a small mesh window was on one side, and an ancient, accordion-style elevator door on the other. Three battered trash cans were the only decoration.

"This is for staff," Mrs. Lattingly explained.

No inlaid marble here.

"This is the only access to the terrace until the tiles are laid." Mrs. Lattingly took the key and fumbled with the dead bolt. "The tiles took forever to get here, six months on a boat from Italy." She jiggled the lock again. "Darn!" She pulled her hand away and stuck a finger in her mouth.

"Allow me, please." Mark took the key in hand and jiggled, then pulled the weight of the door toward him by the handle.

"Careful," Mrs. Lattingly warned. "We had two workers locked out here last week."

Great, Kit thought. She was about to suggest she could come back when the terrace was finished. Or better yet, never.

The old door burst open, bringing in a chilly blast of night air.

Everyone shivered.

Kit thought of her suede trench, hanging in the foyer. Retrieving it would involve walking back through the living room. Great White was there. A little fresh air never hurt anyone, Kit decided. Stepping past them all, she headed into the wintry night—and a black void.

Kit felt around with her foot for the next step and realized, too late, there was none. Flailing her arms wildly, she tried to regain her balance. But there was nothing to grab. No handrails. She tumbled forward.

She landed in a heap at the bottom of a short, steep flight of steps. On her backside. "Ouch!"

"Be careful," Mrs. Lattingly called.

Too late again. Kit did a quick inventory. She had landed at the bottom of cement steps. She had a few scrapes but nothing broken, sprained, or missing, she thought. Her silk stockings were surely shredded. Not too bad, but this was turning out to be the engagement party from hell. Kit smoothed her dress and prepared to stand.

Before she had the chance, Mark sprang down the steps after her. He crouched beside her in the darkness. "Are you okay?" he said.

"Fine."

"Are you sure?" His face loomed over her, frowning with concern.

"Fine, really," Kit murmured. All she wanted now was for this horror show to end. She got her legs underneath her and started to stand.

"Mark! Be careful!" Ruby cried out in the darkness above them. "There's a steep dropoff—"

The rest of her words were lost as the steel door slammed shut. Kit wondered, briefly, why nobody had bothered to warn *her* about the drop. But she had better things to think about. Such as the fact that Mark's face was just inches from hers in the darkness.

"Are you sure you're okay?" he asked.

"Fine. Really." Before Kit could say more, Mark slid one arm beneath her knees and the other behind her back. He scooped her up in one quick motion.

So this is what it feels like to be swept off your feet, For about three seconds, she was cuddled in his arms close to his heart. It felt like the inside of a warm, safe cocoon. "Oh." The sound escaped her lips before she could stop it.

"Okay?"

His voice, low and rumbling, turned Kit's insides to mush. It was a good feeling. She gave a quick nod and for the briefest moment before he set her down she was aware of nothing but the feel of him holding her against him in the darkness. She came to rest gently on her sling-backs. It was a soft landing, as though she was light as a feather, and he didn't groan.

Kit looked up at him. "Er, is your back okay?"

He met her gaze and held it. " 'course."

Kit smiled.

Mark grinned. "I made Eagle Scout, you know."

She giggled. "I guess that makes today my lucky day."

"Don't go spreading it around, okay?"

Kit giggled again as the realization that she was having a good time set in. Despite the fact that she was freezing, and trapped. There were stacks of something blocking access to the rest of the terrace. The custom tumbled tiles from Milan, it appeared. Traffic sounds floated up from Fifth Avenue. Central Park stretched out below, a vast inky carpet of twinkling lights.

"Wow." Mark stood at her side, taking it in.

Kit felt like she was soaring on top of an airplane. She had felt this way before, hiking in the Colorado Rockies. And now, looking out at the famous skyline across the park, topped with a thin sliver of crescent moon the feeling swept over her again. Kit had spent much of her childhood here, but this was the first time she understood how someone could lose heart and soul to New York City.

Mark moved closer to her in the darkness and removed his suit jacket. "You must be frozen." Despite her protest, he wrapped it around her shoulders.

Now she really was inside a safe, warm cocoon.

Someone pounded on the steel door.

Kit could see Ruby's face in the dim window. She was scowling.

"We're stuck," Kit observed.

"I'll get us out of here." Mark reached for Kit again and lifted her off her feet, setting her down in the small space between the mountains of heavy wooden crates and the railing.

Another tingle of excitement coursed through Kit's veins. She had just been swept off her feet for the second time that night, as easily as could be. As though being in Mark's arms was the most natural thing in the world. The thought set off an alarm deep inside her, telling her to run. But there was nowhere to go.

Mark flashed her a Rhett Butler smile and put his hand on her arm. "We'll be okay."

His touch sent a jolt of electricity sizzling through Kit. She could practically hear the circuit breakers popping inside her. She brushed a strand of hair behind one ear, moistened her lips, and tried to speak. "Ah," was the only sound that came out, low and throaty, like the sound she made when she was eating the best dessert imaginable. Kit screwed her eyes shut and gave a quick shake of her head. She shifted her weight inside her snakeskin sling-backs, squared her shoulders, opened her eyes, and willed herself to speak. "Of course we will."

"Don't move."

As if that were possible.

Mark climbed the concrete steps and grabbed the door handle. He yanked on it. Nothing. He yanked again. Nothing. He let go and rubbed his hands. "Let's try this again." He tried once more, throwing his shoulders into it. Still nothing. Mark glared at the door.

He tried again, his breath coming in heavy spurts.

It was a good sound. Kit could listen to it all night, if necessary.

He let go with a grunt. "All that money on tiles and they can't fix the service door." He turned to her. "You okay there?"

"Fine."

"Good."

Ruby yelled. Her words were barely audible through the thick tempered glass of the tiny window set high in the door. "The door is stuck!"

"Whew!" Mark let out a breath and rubbed his hands. "I know," he mouthed to the door. "I'm working on it."

Ruby pouted.

Kit decided she could best help by keeping her mouth shut. She stayed where she was.

Mark gave one last try, to no avail. He eyed the columns of heavy wooden crates that blocked any access to the remainder of the penthouse's wraparound terrace. He put his shoulder to one of the columns and pushed. It barely moved. He stared at the letters on the side of each box and rubbed his chin thoughtfully.

Each crate was clearly stamped in red words, both English and Italian. Kit didn't understand Italian, but the message in English came through loud and clear. *Team lift! Extremely heavy! Fragile as eggs.*

Mark turned to Kit with an appraising look. "Are you any good at climbing?"

Kit's eyes widened in dismay. She glanced around. Wind whipped up off the park, whistling past the heavy columns of crates that crowded the dark terrace. The street below suddenly seemed very distant. She looked at Mark doubtfully.

"The patio's open on the other side of these crates. We can get back inside through one of the sliding doors to the living room. Hopefully in time for pictures," he said, peering at his watch. "Ruby hired a professional photographer."

Kit couldn't be sure whether she'd heard or just imagined a note of exasperation in his voice. But his next words sold her on the climbing idea.

"Maybe we'll get back in before your boss even notices you're gone."

That did it. This was no time for false modesty. "I'm a great climber," Kit said firmly.

Mark looked at her as though she had sprouted wings. "Really?"

"Yup. I grew up in Aspen."

He looked like he had just won the lottery. "Is that a fact?"

"I was a founding member of the Rocky and Bullwinkle Mid-Range Scramblers."

Mark laughed. "Well, all right."

Kit didn't add that the primary requirement for membership was lugging chips, salsa, and a six-pack of beer in her backpack.

Mark smiled so hard his dimple doubled in size. Was he ever cute.

"That makes today my lucky day, too."

"I guess it does."

Ruby pounded on the window again.

Mark motioned at the window. "I'm working on it." He turned back to Kit. "I'll give you a boost. You go over the top of these crates. Drop down the other side and head in through the sliding doors to the living room. Home free."

Kit looked at the mountain of tile crates. It was doable. If they hurried, Mrs. Van Winterden might not even notice her associate editor had been missing for quite a long time.

Mark surveyed the distance from the crates to the railing. "I won't let go till I know you're okay."

"It's a deal."

Mark grinned. "Good girl. Take off your shoes."

Kit felt a tingle of excitement. This might be more fun than she thought.

She kicked off her shoes as Mark laced together his fingers. He hoisted her up slowly, deliberately, carefully.

His jacket slipped from Kit's shoulders. She felt exposed now and tried to ignore it. She searched with her hands for a something to grab. Nothing. Kit shivered. She stretched higher for an edge. Nothing.

"I've got an idea," he said. "Hold on."

Before Kit knew what was happening Mark slipped his head between her legs and boosted her onto his shoulders.

Kit gave a squeal and wrapped both thighs around his neck. She tried to stay calm and get her bearings. "Um, are you okay down there?"

Mark's hands were warm and strong on her bare legs. He tightened his grip.

Kit did a quick mental check. She had changed out of the thong she had worn to the office and slipped on a pair of lace panties and thigh-highs. The 22 Rue St. Honore was still there, on the pulse points at the top of her legs. She always dabbed perfume there, out of habit. And tonight there was someone to appreciate it.

"Um, I'm fine." His voice was muffled. His whiskers grazed her tender skin, setting off a thousand tiny jolts of excitement like shooting stars in the night sky.

Kit drew in a breath and lifted the folds of her dress so he did not suffocate. She looked down and saw the top of his head. His hair was nice and thick. Which struck her as funny. Which unleashed all the nervous energy she felt. She burst into laughter.

Mark shifted his stance, holding steady. He tightened his grip and twisted his head to look at her. "What, may I ask, is so funny?"

Kit was helpless to reply. She couldn't stop laughing.

Mark's mouth twitched. "Don't mind me, but last time I checked this was no laughing matter."

He looked pretty funny with Kit's skirt wrapped around his neck. The sight was too much. Kit laughed harder.

Mark joined in.

Then the door flew open. Mr. Barnard Lattingly, wrench in hand, stepped onto the top step, followed by Ruby and her mother. Mrs. Van Winterden was close behind, flanked by as many guests as could fit.

Kit heard a collective gasp.

Ruby screamed.

Chapter Eight

Weddings, the Van Winterden Way: Keep conversation around the happy couple light and lively.

Ruby screamed and raised both hands to her mouth. "Mark! What are you doing?"

Mr. Lattingly tightened his grip on the wrench. "What the—?"

Mrs. Lattingly placed a warning hand on her husband's arm. "Barney, please." She opened and closed her mouth a few times.

She looked like a fish gasping for air. Mark knew he should do something, anything. But everything was in slow motion, like the time he had broken two ribs in a bad tackle in high school. He lay on the field, unable to move. Like now. He was aware that his guests were gathered around, staring at him.

Kit shifted her weight, reminding him there was a woman perched on his shoulders, her thighs wrapped around his head. He could still smell her scent, warm and floral. A minute ago, they had been laughing together. Mark adjusted his shoulders and blinked, as though there was a spotlight blinding him. He tried to ignore the thought that was pushing its way to the front of his mind. He wanted Kit. Big time. He shook his head.

Ruby seemed to read his mind. She burst into tears, burying her face in her father's jacket.

Kit shifted her legs again, this time insistently. She pushed a hand against his neck and began to slide off.

Mark bent his head to the ground as Kit slid down his shoulders. He caught one more breath of her perfume, fleeting and sweet, like the mood on the terrace up until a minute ago. What the hell was happening to him? "I was trying to find a way for us to get back inside," he said, to Ruby's heaving back.

His in-laws glared at him. He heard tittering from the guests.

Kit smoothed her dress and stared at the ground as though she had lost something and might find it there.

Mark rubbed his neck, trying to think of something to say to end the moment. But all he could think of was how good he had felt until a few minutes ago. The sound of Kit's laughter, the feel of her on his shoulders, the way she smelled. It seemed unreal. But the sound of Ruby's noisy weeping made him feel like a cad. He needed to do something to make her stop. Mark took the steps in a single leap and put his arms around her.

Ruby responded as if someone had asked her to hold a pet boa. Her father had a look that made Mark grateful they were far from the railing. This was bad.

Mrs. Van Winterden cleared her throat. "I suggest we all move inside before someone catches cold."

There was a general shuffling of feet as the guests did an about-face. They wanted to get the heck out of there as badly as he did, Mark thought.

Mrs. Van Winterden whipped a tissue out of nowhere and handed it to Ruby. "Okay, dearie, dry your tears and go inside. Mark will help you freshen up."

Even Ruby wouldn't disobey the schoolteacher tone of voice.

Mrs. Van Winterden was just getting started. "The secret to entertaining well is maintaining a sense of decorum."

Ruby's mother was the first to take the hint. Mark watched in amazement as she peeled Ruby from her father and gave her a small push in Mark's direction. "Barney, inside. We have guests waiting."

Mrs. Van Winterden gave a nod of approval.

Ruby turned to Mark, scowling like a bobcat. Mark placed one arm across her back, which was stiff as an ironing board, and gently steered her inside. He snuck a quick glance back at Kit, who stood shivering.

"You, too, Ms. McCabe." At the sound of her boss's voice, Kit snapped out of it. She thrust her chin up and out. She glanced around and her eyes briefly met Mark's.

Mark winked. None of this was her fault.

Kit gave a tiny, almost imperceptible nod, and quickly walked past his future in-laws and up the steps.

Ruby allowed herself to be steered clear across the penthouse to the master bathroom. It was their preferred spot for arguments at her parents' place.

She whirled on him as soon as he shut the door. "How dare you? Make a scene with that . . . that . . . reporter?"

Mark ducked his head, unable to think of anything to say. He was not a flirt. Not usually. He was as surprised as anyone when he got the urge to lift Kit McCabe onto his shoulders. There was just something about her. She seemed like the type who could take care of herself, relax, and shoot the breeze like one of the guys. Not to mention that she had legs that wouldn't quit, long, sexy red hair, and soft green eyes.

Ruby's voice brought him back to earth. "Do you realize how important tonight is?"

Mark shook his head sadly. "Of course I do."

She held both hands up the sky, palms open, as though asking for help. "My agent is here. And the talent guy from Gotham Productions."

Mark frowned, not sure he understood. It seemed she was more upset about the prospect of losing her cable deal than about him.

"We've been working on this for months. They liked my demo tape. I'm trying to convince them to give me my own show on having it all. And tonight was supposed to prove I know what I'm talking about." Her face crumpled.

The meaning of her words sank in, one by one, like stones sinking to the bottom of a river. Mark felt his stomach tighten. "We'll work it out."

Ruby was now hunched over a plush hand towel crying.

He hated it when women cried. It made him feel helpless, and he would do anything to make that feeling go away. In fact, Mark had agreed to marry Ruby after a crying jag like this one.

"All my friends are getting married! Everyone is married except us!" Ruby had wailed.

Mark had protested they should wait a while, at least so they could plan it. He knew the idea would appeal to Ruby. So he was caught off guard by what she'd told him next.

"The arrangements are already taken care of," she said between sobs. "I entered a contest at *White Weddings* magazine and we won. It's all done, and it's all free."

Mark shook his head. Out of thousands of entries, maybe more, they had chosen his girlfriend as the winner.

"You promised me that our relationship was going somewhere," Ruby had wailed. "It's our one and only chance to have the most fashionable wedding ever, with Ethel Van Winterden and everything. It will be in all the papers. Don't you love me?"

So there it was. Of course he did. And he had always wanted to be married—at some point.

And now here they were, stuck in the bathroom of his future in-laws' penthouse, arguing about the wedding. Again.

Mark ran a hand through his hair. "Sweetie, listen, I don't think we should be taking on so much right now."

Ruby raised her head to glare at him. "How are these reality show people going to hire me when I can't even pull off my own engagement party?"

Mark's stomach tightened. "Locking ourselves in the bathroom won't help."

Ruby dabbed at her eyes and put the towel down, considering his words. "You're right."

Mark thought he had heard wrong.

"We should get out there, top off everyone's drinks and make a joke out of it. Show them I can make the best of a bad situation. We need to show we're a united team." She was thinking out loud now.

Relief washed over him, all the way down to the knot in his stomach. But things still did not seem right as he watched his future bride check her reflection in the mirror. His mind flashed on an image of Kit a short while ago, her eyes filled with wonder at the sight of Central Park by moonlight. Mark closed his eyes.

"Come on, darling," Ruby placed a hand on his arm. "The sooner we get out there, the better. Cheer up. It's over."

Mark opened his eyes and looked at the woman he was going to spend the rest of his life with. Her skin was flawless. There was no evidence she had been crying. She was perfect.

Ruby frowned. "Why are you looking at me like that?"

Mark shook his head. He realized the distant rumble was the sound of blood pumping through his veins. He was close to the edge of something big. It reminded him of how he had felt as a kid, standing at the edge of the high dive right before he jumped.

Judging by the look on her face, Ruby saw it.

Mark knew this was the moment—could be the moment. When he thought of how it would play back later, he winced. "Ruby, this whole thing is just—"

With the sure-footed instincts of a cat, Ruby kissed

him on the lips. Her voice came out in a purr he had not
heard in a long time. "Oh, Mark, this has all been a
whirlwind. We need alone time." She pressed herself
against him so they touched. "I think we should sneak
away for a few days. Just us. We won't tell anybody. We
can use my parents' place in Miami."

Mark opened his mouth to say they didn't need to fly
to Miami to talk, but Ruby placed a finger on his lips.
He sensed his moment was doing a slow fade. He got a
sense of anticlimax, as though he was on the high board
and instead of diving in he was climbing back down the
ladder. His shoulders slumped.

Hours later, as Mark waited for sleep to come, it
wasn't Ruby's face he saw in the darkness. It was Kit's.

After the last toasts had been made, Kit made a get-
away. She pressed the button for the elevator, and prayed
it would come fast. Both knees throbbed, her thigh highs
were history, and her boss was standing beside her.

Kit made a solemn vow that if she survived this elevator ride, she would have nothing more to do with
Mark Dawson. She would say hello, nothing more. She
would interview him for her story, maybe on the telephone, maybe via email. That was it. She snuck a side-
ways glance at Mrs. Van Winterden.

The wedding diva waited silently.

Kit stared at the elevator doors and drew in a deep,
cleansing yoga breath like her mother had taught her. In
through the nose, out through the mouth. It was good
for stress. Many women got through the final stages of
childbirth using this technique. Fingering her belt, Kit

tried to fill her mind with happy images. Flowers in spring, a cloudless sky, puppies.

A small ping sent Kit jumping out of her shoes. So much for yoga breaths. The elevator had arrived, at least.

Mrs. Van Winterden stepped in wordlessly.

Kit followed.

The button marked lobby was already lit. Elevators in luxury buildings were pre-programmed for nonstops to the lobby.

They sank in silence. Kit tried to push away the memory of Mark's hands on her bare legs. It had felt good. Great. Fantastic. But not worth losing her job.

The elevator landed with a thud. Great White stepped off.

Kit counted the steps to the door. Freedom. She could almost taste it.

Great White put on the skids.

Kit almost ran her over. She stopped, waiting.

Great White cleared her throat.

It reminded Kit of a time she had been hiking a valley on the back of Aspen Mountain. She had heard a trickling sound, like water but sharper. She had looked up and seen hundreds of small rocks spilling down the cliff face. It was a miniature avalanche, a mere hint of what could be. The sight had been enough to turn Kit's knees to rubber. The sound of Great White's cough did that now.

The founding editor turned her spectacles toward Kit. "Are you quite all right, Ms. McCabe?"

"Yes." Kit felt she should say something further. "About what happened tonight, on the terrace . . ."

Great White looked at her, expectant.

Kit realized she was offering herself up as easy prey, making this far too easy for her boss, but she plowed ahead anyway. She wanted to keep her job, not become a legend in the editing room. "I want to apologize. That's all."

"The important thing is that you're all right. Correct?"

Kit doubted this was the important thing, but she nodded.

"You lost control of the situation. And that is unfortunate." Mrs. Van Winterden turned to face Kit, full on. "You and I have a contractual obligation to these people. On behalf of our employer."

Employer. The word conjured up a string of related words. *Employment. Job. Jobless. Unemployed. Fired.*

Great White watched Kit, as though she could see into Kit's stomach and knew the effect of her words there. "We must never forget that our behavior is a reflection on this magazine and our employers."

Kit felt a swelling in her throat that marked the beginning of a sob. She looked at a spot on her shoes, horrified.

"You were chosen over a number of qualified writers for this assignment."

Kit pictured a pack of editors, howling like wolves in the wilderness.

"Any one of them would jump at the chance to work with me on this project."

Kit waited. Here it came.

"I think we need to review your performance first thing tomorrow morning. Half past seven. In my office."

That was it. Kit realized it wasn't Great White's style

to fire somebody in the lobby of an apartment building, even one as grand as this. No, she preferred to do it back in her lair. Kit nodded, signaling she understood. She blinked back hot tears of embarrassment. She wished she'd never been chosen for this assignment. Maybe she could go back to Colorado and lead white-water rafting trips like her best friend from grade school.

Mrs. Van Winterden waved off the doorman's offer to hail a cab.

She lived just a few short steps away, Kit knew, in a penthouse as splendid as the one they just had left.

"Enjoy your evening, Ms. McCabe." Without waiting for a reply, Great White vanished into the night.

Chapter Nine

*Weddings, the Van Winterden Way: Short engagements
are advisable.*

Kit did not sleep well. She had a nightmare that she
was drowning in a sea of ivory tulle. Her throat closed
and she woke up, gasping for air. Her allergies were
back. She tossed and turned until dawn, making a vow
that if she managed to keep her job after today she
would have as little to do with Mark as humanly possible. With any luck, she'd be taken off this cover story.
She again dressed in her best navy suit, and reported to
Mrs. Van Winterden's office at exactly eighteen minutes past seven.

One look at the founding editor's face told her the
meeting wasn't going to take long.

Great White motioned for Kit to sit. "Let's get right to
the point. Your behavior does not befit this publication."

Kit gulped.

"Despite the fact that there were other, more qualified editors for this assignment, we chose you. None of
them were available."

Ouch. Kit noticed a small fleck of dust somehow had
been allowed to settle on the polished mahogany desk.
It didn't belong there. It was as much out of place, apparently, as was Kit McCabe's name on the masthead
of the magazine.

"Luckily, some schedules have shifted and one of
my senior editors is now available."

Kit's heart fell down all the way to her feet. She'd
been expecting these words, but hearing them still hurt
more than she had imagined.

"Your behavior has upset Miss Lattingly, Mr. Dawson, their family and friends."

An unanticipated force pulled down the corners of
Kit's mouth, and she realized with horror she was about
to cry.

"Frankly, I can see no reason to keep you on this assignment."

Kit's tongue was glued to the roof of her mouth,
which tasted of gun metal. Misery had a taste. Who
knew? She realized her career was slipping away. In
another ninety seconds, or maybe less, it would be over.
She couldn't bear it. She had just one more chance. She
seized it with all the desperation a drowning man shows
for a life preserver. Her voice came out sounding weak,
but serious. "I have an idea."

Great White's eyebrows shot up so high they practically disappeared into her coif.

"Mrs. Lattingly and I discussed an idea for a feature article for *The Feathered Nest.* She's very keen on a story about her condo in Miami. I told her I could work something up, and she was very pleased." Of course that was before she caught her future son-in-law wearing Kit like a muffler around his neck.

"Good work." Mrs. Van Winterden made a temple with her fingers. "I'll have someone from *The Feathered Nest* assigned to it."

"I've already spoken to Edgar Lacey, and he's assigned it to me." A complete, bold-faced lie.

Great White's eyes narrowed.

Kit barreled on. There was no point stopping now. "The Lattinglys will be very pleased if we feature their condo in *The Feathered Nest.* And if I'm the one who does it, it's the best form of damage control. I think the best thing for the magazine is to improve the existing relationship."

Mrs. Van Winterden leaned back, removed her glasses, and massaged a red spot on the bridge of her nose.

Great White sniffed. She replaced her glasses. "Frankly, Ms. McCabe, I am at a loss as to how to salvage the relationship with the Lattinglys right now," she sighed. "You are correct, however. The most important thing right now is to undo some of the damage you've caused. I agree the home décor article is a good idea."

Kit sat up straighter.

Great White watched her, eyes narrowed. "And I think it's best if you leave town for a few days."

Kit's breath exited her lungs with a quick whoosh, leaving an empty space behind. She felt hollow. But it sounded as if she still had a job. And a trip to Miami might be just the thing to get Mark Dawson off her mind.

Mrs. Van Winterden placed her hands on her desk and pushed herself back.

The matter was settled.

"Edgar Lacey is working on a new concept for *The Feathered Nest,* one that will show how much can be accomplished by someone with a design challenge, a limited budget, and no special talent."

Great White paused, no doubt to give Kit time to ponder how well she fit the requirements, particularly "no special talent." Kit shifted in her seat and willed herself not to check her watch.

"When you turn in the final copy and proofs," Mrs. Van Winterden continued, "We'll see where we stand with regard to the cover story for *White Weddings.*"

The cover story for *White Weddings.* Not *your* cover story for *White Weddings.* But there was nothing more she could do. Kit nodded.

"I'll need to see the finished article by day's end Monday."

It was an impossible deadline to meet. Kit tried not to flinch. "No problem."

Great White was quiet, as if she was surprised Kit hadn't quit just then. She smiled with her mouth closed and signaled with a wave of one doll-sized hand that the meeting was over.

Kit rose to leave.

"Ms. McCabe, let's be clear on something. I want to

be called immediately if anything goes wrong. Use my pager. Understood?"

Kit nodded. She braced herself for what she knew was coming. It came.

"I would prefer that you keep your personal life private."

Kit looked down at her navy pumps, mortified. "Right. Thank you for . . . for everything." She glanced back up.

Great White had already swiveled away.

Kit raced down to Edgar's office, knocked once and barged in. She explained everything, including the fact that Mrs. Van Winterden had told her about Edgar's new column, which meant that now he was Kit's only hope. Not to mention her best friend in the entire world.

"Not a chance." Edgar shook his head.

"But you said you'd do anything to help."

"I lied."

"My job is on the line." Kit was pleading now.

"Sweetie, I don't want to save your job if it means putting mine on the line. I'll be a laughing stock if I run a photo spread of some ugly condo whose owners just happen to be the parents of the woman who won our wedding sweepstakes. What you should do," his voice dropped a notch, "is just plan a weekend down there with lover boy."

Kit shook her head. Why couldn't everyone just forget all about this and move on? "There's nothing between us. What happened at the party last night was just a silly, stupid terrace malfunction."

Edgar laughed. "Terrace malfunction? Cookie.

Please. The guy follows you onto a terrace in the dark. And there, right in front of his in-laws, not to mention his bride, hoists you up over his head." He paused here for effect. "And, honey, I know what you weigh."

Kit glared at him.

"He swings you onto his shoulders. And you don't think there's something going on there? He's obviously got a thing for you. You've got a thing for him. Why not check it out? Call him and tell him this time he's won a free trip. To Miami. With you."

"Edgar, you need to get this." Kit raised both hands, palms facing each other, to place an imaginary bracket around her words for emphasis. "There is nothing between me and Mark. Nothing. Nada. Niente. Zip."

Edgar did the pouty thing he sometimes did with his lips. The expression on his face said, "Yeah, right."

Kit sighed. Not even her best friend believed her.

They stared at each other for a moment in a kind of Mexican standoff. Edgar leaned in closer, serious now. "You know, Kit, you don't want to go through life always writing about other people's weddings. Some day, you need to plan one of your own. And for that, you're going to have to open yourself up."

Kit felt her mouth settle in a straight line, based on long years of practice spent shuttling from coast to coast for alternating holidays with her parents. The pain wasn't as sharp as it used to be, but it was still there. Like a root canal gone bad. Aching. Ready to flare again.

Edgar reached out and gave Kit's shoulder a quick squeeze. "I'm here for you, Kit, okay?"

Tears pooled in her eyes. She ducked her head so Edgar wouldn't see and swiped them with her wrist.

Edgar offered his sleeve, the ultimate sacrifice.

She pushed it away, gently declining his offer, and smiled. The tension between them was gone. "What I need to do is get back on track with *her,*" Kit said with a glance in the direction of Mrs. Van Winterden's office suite.

Edgar gave Kit the sort of look a teacher might give his favorite student who has just refused to do her algebra. "Okay. We'll do it your way, Cookie. It's only time you're wasting."

Was it Kit's imagination, or was everyone starting to talk like Mother's Lama? She let out a breath, exasperated. "Look, if I can keep my job by pulling an all-nighter, or whatever it takes, I'll do it. Give me a chance. Please." She was pleading and she knew it.

"You'll need to pull more than one all-nighter," Edgar said, in a warning tone. "More like three."

Which meant he'd give her the assignment. Kit jumped to her feet, raced around the desk and gave Edgar a giant bear hug, Colorado-style. "Thank you, thank you, thank you." She allowed herself to feel a tiny bit of relief. She was worn out with worry, tired of strategizing, and her knees were covered with bruises. And it was not yet 8:00 A.M. "You're a pal, you know?"

Edgar grinned. "I do. But let the record show, I won't be truly happy until I dance at your wedding."

Kit shot him a look. "Let's get one thing straight. I will have nothing further to do with Mark Dawson. He's going to get married and go on his merry way. Nothing to do with me. Nothing."

There was silence as Edgar gave her his if-you-say-so look. Strangling him was out of the question. She needed his help. "Now, can we please talk about business?"

"Okay," he said with a harumph. "At least that's something we can agree on."

Kit felt her heart melt as he explained her piece would be used in "Rough Cuts," a new column about do-it-yourself home makeovers featuring a limited budget and no special skills on the part of the designer. The column was his brainchild, his baby. He had lobbied hard for months to get the publishers to agree to it. And Kit's article about the Lattingly condo would be the debut column in next month's issue. If she turned it in on time.

Kit was so full of gratitude she didn't know what to say. She felt tears fill her eyes, and fought to hold them back. The last thing he needed was a weepy freelancer in charge of his baby. When she spoke her voice was solemn. "Edgar, I promise I'll turn the piece in on time. And it will be perfect."

Edgar nodded. He looked worried.

Kit knew she needed to go the extra mile. She extended her pinky finger.

Edgar hooked his pinky around Kit's with a quick nod. "Good luck, Cookie. And, whatever you do, don't screw this up."

"Thanks, friend." She was going to need the luck. Hers wasn't the only job on the line now. Edgar's was, too. Thanks to her.

Mark arrived at work early, while the office was still quiet. There was nobody crowding onto the elevator or standing around the kitchenette waiting for the coffee to brew. Nobody ribbing him about his engagement party last night. He slammed the door to his office behind him anyway.

An envelope on top of his in box was marked "Courier express." He knew from the return address it was from the travel agent. Inside were two First Class tickets to Miami, departing tonight.

He tried to work, but Kit's face made it impossible to concentrate. The way she had looked when she walked into that party last night. Sharp as a tack in a black dress that was just tight enough to show her curves. Long red hair, green eyes and full lips. When she smiled, her whole face lit up. Her scent still lingered in his mind, soft and sweet. The thought of it made him shut his eyes, and left him breathless.

The physical sensation was distracting. He couldn't work like this. Shifting in his chair, he stared at the computer and tried to concentrate but it was no use. He had to talk to Kit. Just to make sure she still had a job after last night. She was a cool customer, but her boss did not look like she had become the wedding diva by cutting anyone any slack. It was a courtesy call. Nothing more.

Mark pulled Kit's card from his Rolodex and dialed the number. He got voicemail and hung up. He ran a hand through his hair, thinking. He couldn't rest until he heard her voice. He dialed information and got a residence listing for McCabe, initial *K*, in Manhattan. No street address. Which was good. Single girls always did that so creepy guys could not find out where they lived. Mark dialed the number and heard her voice on the answering machine. Also good. No live-in boyfriend there. He hung up again without leaving a message.

She was not at home. Good sign. She was at work, head down—unless she had been sacked. In which case she was at home with the covers pulled over her head, watching talk shows to drown out her sorrows. Mark stared at his computer screen and tried to concentrate. When all else failed, he checked his email. But he pushed the mouse away, unable to shake the idea of Kit losing her big cover story, sitting at home, crying her little eyes out. And it was his fault.

Mark jumped to his feet, threw on his overcoat and told the admin he had a dentist appointment. He headed out, hailed a cab and directed the driver to take the West Side Highway uptown to the headquarters of *White Weddings* magazine.

Kit raced off the elevator, past the waterfalls and towering coconut trees that dotted the award-winning atrium of *White Weddings* magazine offices. She checked her watch. If all went well, she would have just enough time to grab a few things at home and catch the noon nonstop to Miami. The call to Mrs. Lattingly had gone off without a hitch. Ruby's mother was quick to forgive Kit once she found out her winter home would be featured in the next swank issue of *The Feathered Nest*. In fact her voice oozed like honey by the end of the call. "You can collect the key to the condo from the managing agent on your way to the beach, my dear. I'll call and advise them you're on your way."

Kit hurried through the giant revolving doors and stepped out onto Sixth Avenue. If she worked hard and didn't sleep much over the next few days, she might just save her job—and forget all about Mark Dawson in the process. That would be a bonus.

The first hint of spring was in the air, luring crowds of office workers onto the street. Kit scowled. It would be tough to find a cab.

North bound traffic was at a crawl. Kit saw lots of cabs but they were all occupied. She'd have better luck on a side street. She trudged over to West Forty-sixth Street with a firm grasp on her pocketbook, camera bag, briefcase, laptop, and bottle of sunblock, SPF 50. The last was a parting gift from Edgar, with a warning to stay out of the midday sun. As if she would have time for sun. She had just rounded the corner when a cab pulled to the curb right in front of her.

It was the sort of miracle that makes a New Yorker smile. Kit waved frantically and closed in. She might just make her flight. The back door swung open, and she heard a familiar voice from inside. "Keep the change."

That voice, mellow and deep, unleashed a torrent of butterflies in Kit's stomach. It was getting to be a habit, but she was not growing used to it. The sounds and movement of Midtown faded around her as Mark Dawson stepped out of the cab. It was as if the earth had stopped rotating. He got out without glancing around and then, ever the gentleman, held the door open. "All yours. Do you need a hand?" he said before looking up. Then he saw who had been waiting for his cab.

Something tangible passed between them in that moment of recognition, like the stillness just before a lightening bolt strikes, searing the landscape forever. She could almost smell the ozone. Kit felt she had known him forever.

Mark swallowed hard, his Adam's apple climbing high above his collar, and she was certain he felt it, too. "Hi, Kit."

She loved the way her name sounded on his lips. She wondered if he felt the same pleasure at seeing her. "Hi, Mark."

He broke into a big, wide smile that lit up his entire face, During which time the butterflies in her stomach whipped into a whirling cloud. Mark cleared his throat. "I wanted to drop by, to see how things were going for you—at work."

Of course. He must have thought she had been fired. How pathetic. Kit's cheeks flushed. "I'm fine, no problem." She looked down and ran the toe of her shoe along the sidewalk. She felt a few strands of hair blowing freely in the soft spring breeze, and pushed them back behind one ear. She glanced up.

He reached out to touch her.

Whether he wanted to brush her hair back or help with her bags, Kit wasn't sure. She stepped back as though she were avoiding a hunter's trap. She had spent the morning doing everything she could think of to hold on to her job, and having anything at all to do with Mark would put her back in jeopardy. "I'm fine," she said in her best all-business tone. She didn't dare meet his eyes. "I've got to run."

His face took on a hangdog look, sending Kit's stomach butterflies back to roost. A passerby made a move for the cab. "You taking this?"

Mark brightened. "Help yourself."

Kit, however, wasn't giving up. "It's taken." She grabbed the door handle.

The stranger frowned. "You staying or going?"

"Going." Kit tossed her bags on the back seat.

The man stomped off.

As Kit slid into the back seat, Mark put his hand on the door, brushing hers. He lowered his face close to hers, so she could see the flecks of gold in his brown eyes.

All of Kit's senses went to a state of heightened alert. Her skin tingled from head to toe, and the heat she'd felt last night was back, rising from deep inside. Her breath caught in her throat, and her heart raced. She tried to swallow, but found it difficult. If she moved her hand an inch, it would touch his.

He watched her closely, his face inches from hers. His jaw worked furiously, as though there was a war going on inside him. When he spoke, his voice was low and restrained. "Look, I wanted to see how you're doing. And I'm sorry." He moved his hand, spreading his fingers as if to show he was sorry about many things.

Kit knew better than to speak. A wave of emotion swept over her like a tidal wave. If she was not careful, she would drown. She looked away, gathering her thoughts. "Don't worry about it. It wasn't your fault."

He gave a small nod, his jaw still working like he wanted to say more. But he didn't.

That settled it for Kit. She tried to sound confident, even though she didn't feel that way. "What happened last night is no big deal. Things are fine for me at work. No harm done." If she could manage to do with no sleep at all in the next two days, to work around the clock on a photo shoot that would give new meaning to the term "Rough Cuts," and manage to deliver a perfect feature article to one of the most demanding editors in the business, she might manage to hang on to her job.

Mark gave her a look that said, "Okay, if you say so."

"Thanks for checking on me," Kit said in her best 'places-to-go-people-to-see' tone of voice. *Good luck with your wedding. Have a nice life.*

Mark nodded, pulling his lips into a tight smile.

Kit gently tugged at the door. If she hurried, she could still make her flight and keep her job. And he could still have his celebrity wedding.

"Right," he said. He did not look happy.

A horn blared behind them. Kit pulled the door shut, clutching her belongings against her. She was going to make this flight if it killed her. If she missed it, Edgar would kill her.

Patting the door, Mark straightened up. "I'll be seeing you."

Kit nodded.

The cab pulled away but gained only a short distance before stopping for a red light, making Kit groan aloud. Right now she wanted to get as far away from Mark as possible before she changed her mind and ran back to tell him how she really felt. Thereby making a complete fool of herself in front of someone else's fiancé. Kit sank back against the seat, not daring to look back.

If she had looked back, she would have seen Mark standing where she'd left him, rubbing his jaw thoughtfully.

Chapter Ten

Weddings, the Van Winterden Way: A pre-wedding get-away is recommended.

Kit made good time at her apartment, madly tossing summer clothes into a suitcase. She added a black bikini on top. She was going to South Beach, after all.

The phone rang. Kit assumed it was the car service, a few minutes ahead of schedule, picked up, and heard static on the line. It was a happy sound. Kit choked up and sank down onto the couch. "Mom?"

Her mother's voice floated through the phone lines like a long-distance hug. Things were fine in Nepal. The macrobiotic diet was working wonders, and the entire ashram was having spiritual awakenings all over the place. "How are things with you?" she asked.

"Okay." Kit's voice broke before the word left her lips. She burst into tears.

"Doesn't sound that way," her mother said, sympathetically. "Want to tell me about it?"

"It's this darned assignment."

Her mother chuckled softly, "Darned assignment? I take it things aren't going according to plan?"

Things were Mark Dawson, to be precise. "No." Kit let the tears fall, finally.

"Kit, you're very good at what you do. And besides, your big article isn't due for another week or two."

Mother might be trekking through rhododendrons on the far side of the planet, but she did not miss much. "I just, I just . . . ," Kit hesitated, not sure how to say it. "It's the groom."

There was a pause on the other end of the phone. "Does he have a name?"

"Mark Dawson." Saying it filled Kit with warmth.

"Want to tell me about him?"

Kit closed her eyes, not even sure how to begin. "He's all wrong for her."

There was a buzz on the intercom. Kit's car service had arrived.

Mother chuckled softly, "I see."

"This whole assignment is turning out to be harder than I thought." It was the understatement of the century. Kit sniffled. "No matter what I do, I can't make it turn out okay. There was a scene the other night, and now I've got to go to Miami, and I just don't know if I can do all this."

"So, the assignment is all wrong?"

Kit drew a breath in wearily. This was where she was supposed to see the light, admit everything.

The buzzer sounded again, longer this time.

Kit closed her eyes. "I can't go into details, because I've got to run. Honestly, I'm not sure I'll have a job this time next week."

"Everything's okay, sweet girl."

Kit shook her head. A tear slipped out. "You don't understand. And I'm so tired, I don't know which end is up."

"More will be revealed," her mother said gently.

Kit winced. There it was. Lama wisdom.

"I mean it, Kit. More will be revealed. Everything is fine just the way it is. If you're feeling anxious, it's because you need to be honest with yourself. You will be, and until then the universe will keep pushing you along."

Kit checked her watch and stood. Time may move slowly in Katmandu, or at base camp in the Himalayas, or wherever Mother was. But Kit had a plane to catch.

"Thanks, Mom."

"Kit, I want to tell you one thing before you rush off. This job and the feelings you have are only an illusion. If you feel out of control and tired, it means you've been presented with a core issue from your psychic drama."

Kit walked toward the door, collecting her overcoat on the way, suddenly anxious to leave.

"If you're tired, it means you're fighting your true feelings. One of your chakras is blocked."

Kit rolled her eyes.

"You'll feel better when you face your feelings."

Conversations like this were the reason Kit turned to her father when she wanted career guidance. But at least her mother wasn't the sort who was always asking if she had met anyone. "Thanks, Mom."

"You're facing a psychic challenge. And it's probably not the one you think."

Kit fingered the end call button and checked her watch. "Thanks, Mom."

"You run along, Sweetie. And I'll ask the universe to clear a path for you. Don't worry, your karma is being revealed."

Kit wiped her tears. Her mother meant well. "Sounds good, Mom. You do that." Later, she would wonder if the Himalayas had a clear signal to the great beyond.

Kit made it to La Guardia on time, and spent the flight scouring recent copies of the *Feathered Nest* and *Architectural Digest* for inspiration on trends—and to push aside thoughts of Mark Dawson. Why, she could not help but wonder, had she waited her entire life to meet the right man only to find him after he was already engaged to someone else?

Kit picked up her rental car at Miami airport and within minutes was zooming east on Route 836 to Miami Beach. Her hair blew in the breeze. She felt the hot sun on her skin, tuned the radio to a salsa station, and watched for signs to the MacArthur Causeway. There were all manner of pleasure craft plying the waters of Biscayne Bay. Sailboats skimmed the waves and motorboats sped along. Fishermen lined the walkways on either side of the bridge.

Kit headed onto the barrier island, making a quick stop to collect the key from the managing agent of the

Lattinglys' condo. She found Collins Avenue, the main drag, and headed north. To her left were pastel mansions to her right the Atlantic sparkled in the mid-day sun like countless diamonds.

Kit found the Lattinglys' building, a tall high-rise with a private beach. A blast of air-conditioning hit her as soon as she entered the lobby. She took the elevator to one of the higher floors and found the door, anxious to see what awaited her inside.

She opened the door, took one look, and her heart sank. The living room was white, with furniture of chrome and glass, beige carpeting, and white blinds obscuring the ocean view.

Kit felt her mood drop as she walked through to the master bedroom. It was about as welcoming as a furniture showroom. The bathroom, with its giant hot tub, was done in white marble. Kit shivered. She needed to find a theme for her "Rough Cuts" piece. "White-Out" was all that came to mind.

Kit looked around. It was hard to imagine Mark here. *Mark.* There he was again, all warm brown eyes and strong hands, invading her mind. Kit massaged her temples and closed her eyes, trying to focus. But she couldn't fight the thought of how exciting it would be if he were here with her, right now, What if he were here? Kit opened her eyes and looked around with fresh vision. *Zen and the Art of Condo Decorating.* What would this condo look like if she were designing a cozy getaway for Mark?

The idea gave new interest to the king-size bed, the roomy hot tub, and the sound of ocean waves pounding outside. She could turn the condo into a cozy love nest. *Miami a deux.*

Kit smiled as the idea took root and blossomed. Possibilities abounded. Zen was a good thing. Score one for Mother and her Lama. But now Kit had to make it happen. She sprang into action. Her work was cut out for her.

Mark arrived at La Guardia late that afternoon. He checked in for his Miami flight at the First Class counter, only to learn Ruby hadn't yet arrived. He looked at his watch. She'd better get here quick if she was going to make the flight.

He dialed her cell phone. It went straight to voice mail.

He headed to the gate and found a seat. The hours had passed slowly since he had seen Kit that morning. *Kit.* He couldn't stop thinking about her. She had frozen him out today. And who could blame her? He was getting married next week. So, why could he not stop thinking about her?

Mark glanced at his watch. Ten minutes had passed. Where the heck was Ruby? She was late as a rule, but this was pushing it, even for her. Someone had left a copy of the *New York Post* lying on the seat next to him, and he flipped through it to pass the time. An item in the "Page Six" gossip column caught his eye:

We're in the home stretch for next week's White Weddings-*sponsored sweepstakes nuptials. Our sources tell us Ruby's dress is to die for. And why not? It was designed just for her and, we hear, will have to be sewn on. Watch the calories, girlfriend.*

*Because we hear if all goes well she'll ink a deal
for her own cable show "Having It All," the gal's
guide to landing the perfect man, job, and apartment in New York. Who knows better than Ruby
Lattingly? We hear she's close to signing with
Fresh, the agency that launched a thousand faces.
Not to mention she just landed one of Gotham's
hunkiest bachelors, and a free wedding to boot.
You go, girl! Lucky Mark Dawson. He's taken
Gotham by storm, with the perfect job, the perfect
girl, and now a free wedding with all the trimmings, and all he has to do is show up on time.
Now, that's "Having It All."*

Mark frowned, flipped the paper shut and tossed it
back onto the seat. There was no escaping the *White
Weddings* P.R. machine. He felt like a cog in a wheel
that was spinning out of control. He again glanced at
his watch, now irritated.

His cell phone rang.

Ruby's voice sounded breezy, for a change. Which
was a good thing. Her words, however, were anything
but. "Darling—tonight—tomorrow—sorry."

He could make out only half of what she said, no
thanks to a weak signal. "What?"

"Cable—" There was a pause, then more static.
Ruby said something about her agent. "—sorry."

A voice boomed over the PA system, announcing the
flight to Miami was ready to board.

Mark pressed the cell phone closer to his head, and
stuck a finger in his free ear.

"Big—perfect event—modeling." Ruby's voice, shrill with excitement, screeched through the phone. But her words kept breaking up.

Mark hunched over the phone as the First Class passengers began boarding.

Ruby chirped away, "—tomorrow night."

The line went dead.

Mark held the phone in his hand for a moment, studying it. Then shrugged. Ruby was not coming—at least not till tomorrow night, by the sound of it. He felt relieved. This whole thing had been her idea of a romantic getaway weekend.

The gate agent who had checked him in earlier was now motioning him to get on board.

This weekend had been Ruby's idea—just like the wedding. What Mark needed was a break from all of it. The wedding, the contest and Ruby. The realization hit him with the force of a full body check. Mark made up his mind.

He stowed his cell phone, gathered his belongings, and walked quickly to board his flight.

Kit felt a tingle of joy. The transformation of the Lattingly condo was complete. She had shopped for accent pieces and placed them strategically around the white furniture. Colorful pillows and tasseled throws now dressed the sofa and chairs, and swags of peach-colored sheers warmed the windows that were now flung open to capture the warm ocean breeze. A few beaded lamps lent a soft light. The overall effect was warm and inviting.

The bedroom was dramatic. The large bed was

worthy of a harem. Angled into a corner and framed with cascading silk greenery and flowers, the headboard was draped with generous folds of velour nearly covered by mountains of softly ruffled pillows. Scented, slow-burning candles of genuine beeswax twinkled merrily, casting a warm glow and the scent of gardenias about the room. Jazz played softly on the stereo.

The master bedroom was now a playground for two.

The patio was set for a romantic dinner of *carne asada* and rice, with a salad of organic greens and, in honor of all her hard work, a bottle of Chablis chilling on ice.

Most important, she had stayed within the parameters of the "Rough Cuts" rule by transforming the space with no professional help, very little time, and a budget of no more than five hundred dollars. Luck had been with her. The afternoon light had been perfect as Kit had raced from room to room with a local freelance photographer to shoot each room from every possible angle. The photographer was to email Edgar a full range of digital shots. Kit would write the accompanying copy once she was back at her desk in New York. And the Lattinglys would be able to keep the accent pieces if they wished. The hard part was done, and with any luck, Kit could turn the article in on time.

Her plan was to stay overnight and catch the early flight to JFK in the morning. Mrs. Lattingly's mood had improved so much she'd insisted Kit stay in the condo since nobody would be using it this close to the Ruby's wedding. Edgar had liked the idea, since it would save the hit on his budget for the cost of a hotel room in Miami in high season.

Kit's sore muscles cried for the tub. She had earned a good long soak before dinner. She ran a bath of warm water, sprinkled it with scented oils, and stripped off her sweaty clothes, tossing them in the closet. The soft night air felt good on her bare skin as she moved through the condo, switching off all the lights.

She lowered her body into the scented water of the giant tub and felt the stress of the last few days drain away. The effect was heavenly.

There was nothing better than Miami, Mark thought, especially on a soft, warm night like this, and when it had been raining slush back in New York. And most especially when he needed a break. The wedding seemed a thousand years and a million miles off. But Kit McCabe did not. She had taken up residence in his mind, and didn't seem ready to move out any time soon. Mark looked out at the running lights of a power boat in the bay as he drove across the causeway. In one week's time, he would be married.

He pulled into the parking lot of his future in-laws' condo just before 9:00 P.M. He was hungry. He thought he would grab a quick shower and change before heading out for a bite to eat. He fished in his pocket for Ruby's key as he headed inside, grateful for some time on his own. A night down here, away from Ruby and the whole wedding thing, should put things in perspective, he thought.

He had no idea how right he was.

*   *   *

Kit felt the tension leave her mind and body. The jets in the tub rumbled softly, pulsing warm and silky water against her skin. A tiny beaded lamp shed soft light on the newly-purchased wicker baskets overflowing with plush cotton terry towels. Thick looped rugs warmed the floor and steps leading up to the giant tub lined with seashells and flickering votive candles. Small wire containers held silk ivy, scented soaps, and bath oils. Fresh rose petals were strewn about, a remnant of the day's photo shoot.

She drew in a couple of deep breaths and closed her eyes, letting herself drift into a state of complete relaxation. She could have stayed in the tub all night but her stomach rumbled, reminding her she hadn't eaten anything since the tiny bag of peanuts on the plane.

She got out and toweled off, wrapping one of the plush oversized towels around her hair and another around her body. She was looking around for her slippers when a small sound—or perhaps it was just a feeling—made her straighten up and look toward the door.

She couldn't believe what she saw.

He was there. Mark Dawson. In the flesh. Standing in the doorway, his eyes open wide with a mixture of utter shock and something else that would nag at her until she had time to sort things out in her mind much later.

He had already taken off his shirt, no doubt planning to take a bath himself. He was naked from the waist up, his chest and stomach sleek and smooth with muscles like a model in an Abercrombie & Fitch ad.

Mark's hand froze as he was reaching to unbuckle his belt.

She clutched the towel more tightly about her and screamed.

Chapter Eleven

Weddings, The Van Winterden Way: Allow time for the couple to pursue common interests.

Kit drew herself up to her full height, gasped and stared at Mark, indignant. When she found her voice, a single word squeaked out. "You!"

Mark backed up a step. His gaze swept the room, taking in the tub, the flickering candles, and rose petals before coming to rest on the oversized towel Kit was clutching around her like armor. He shook his head in amazement, swallowed with an effort that was audible, sending his Adam's apple higher up his throat. His voice was low and husky. "I didn't know anyone was here."

In a brief instant of insanity, Kit's heart had leaped at the possibility that Mark had followed her, had sought her out. But of course that was impossible. Kit folded her arms more firmly across her midsection. "What are you doing here?"

"I needed to get away, and I thought the place would be empty," he said apologetically.

Kit couldn't blame him for that. She nodded.

A look of realization transformed his face as he glanced again at the twinkling candles and rose petals all around. "I'm sorry. I'll get out of here. You might be expecting . . ." his voice trailed off before he finished the sentence. As though it were the most natural thing in the world that Kit would be entertaining someone in his future in-law's bathtub.

She said curtly, "I certainly am not." Her eyes blazed at the suggestion.

"Sorry," he said quickly. But the look he gave her was quizzical.

"It's just me," she explained.

His eyebrows shot up. He ran his tongue across his lips and swallowed again with difficulty. "I'm sorry," he said again.

She was really embarrassed now, and still hugging herself tightly. "I came down to do a photo shoot."

He met her gaze again, careful to keep his eyes fixed above her neck.

Ever the gentleman, Kit thought. It only made her like him more.

But Mark couldn't stop the smile from playing around his lips. "What sort of photo shoot?"

Kit tried in vain to sound as official as possible. "Home décor. Romantic makeovers. It's for *The Feathered Nest.*"

"I see," he said with a nod. A big smile spread slowly across his face and he looked away. "Uh, I love what you've done with the place."

She could practically hear the twinkle in his eye. Kit felt her cheeks turn what was certain to be a neon shade of red. She needed to get out of this bathroom, this condo, and the entire state of Florida. "Thanks. Now, out."

"Right." He turned quickly and, stopping to collect his shirt from where he had tossed it on the floor, left the bedroom suite, closing the door gently behind him.

Kit went into the master bedroom, where the strains of jazz music still wafted faintly through the air. She shrugged off the towels and pulled on her knit travel pantsuit. She tossed her other things into her suitcase and zipped it. If she hurried, she could catch the last flight to New York. She took one last look at herself in one of the floor-length mirrors that lined the closet doors. Her red hair tumbled in damp ringlets around her neck. She needed to get out of here. Now.

She walked briskly out to the living room to say good-bye. Mark wasn't there. The galley kitchen was empty as well, Which left the terrace.

There, he was, standing at the rail, looking out to sea. He was bathed in silver under the light of an honest-to-goodness full moon. The sight of him tugged at something in her. She felt all her molecules rearranging themselves as one, pushing her toward him like the tide.

She held back, clearing her throat to let him know she was there.

He turned, his eyes dark as night. He had put his shirt back on and buttoned it, though not all the way to the top. A few chest hairs peeked out, giving a hint of what was underneath.

She saw his eyes take in everything from the tips of her toes to her tousled hair and felt a warm flush of pleasure pass over her skin. She marveled at the effect he had on her, stronger each time she saw him.

"So," he finally said.

"So," she said at the same time.

He smiled. "Here we are on a balcony again."

Kit could not help but smile back. Even though the last place she should be was alone with Mark on a balcony under the light of a full moon.

His expression turned serious. "Sorry I barged in on you."

Kit gave a shake of her head. "It's okay. I had no idea you were going to be here." *If I had, it's the last place on earth I would have come.*

"Nobody knew. I," he paused, searching for the right word, "er, we, decided to come down for the weekend. Nobody knew."

We. Small word. Two letters. It hit Kit like a blast of arctic air. "Is Ruby . . . ?"

"She's coming down tomorrow night," Mark said quietly. "We, er, she wanted us to have a weekend away. But then she needed to cancel at the last minute. She had a big meeting with her agent and a producer and couldn't get away. We'll have a good time when she gets here." His shoulders sagged.

"Yeah," Kit said, "that sounds great." Her voice lacked enthusiasm and she knew it. But she hated to see the tightness in his jaw. "You'll both have a great time once she gets here," she added, and meant it.

"Yeah," he said with a small smile. But the tightness in his jaw remained and he couldn't hold back a sigh.

"It'll be good to be away, just the two of us . . . remind us why we're doing all this." He looked out to sea and jangled the change in his pocket the way Kit's father sometimes did when he was uncomfortable. Perhaps he felt he had said too much.

"Planning a big wedding can be overwhelming," Kit said helpfully.

He nodded and turned to her. "Sometimes I feel as though I'm stuck on a speeding train and I can't stop it. You ever feel like that?"

Only since I've met you. Kit nodded wordlessly, sensing he needed to talk.

He sighed, absently running a hand through his hair. "Nothing feels right about this entire wedding, if you want to know the truth. Don't get me wrong, you and Mrs. Van Winterden and the magazine have been great," he said quickly.

Kit shrugged. "It's okay."

"It's just . . . ," he paused, shaking his head. "I've heard of pre-wedding jitters. I guess everybody gets them."

"Yeah." Kit fought the urge to grab his arms and yell at him to get out while he had the chance. Spending the rest of his life with Ruby would be like living on a glacier, perched on a permanent ice shelf that no amount of global warming could melt. "Things will work out exactly the way they're meant to," she said, trying to sound hopeful. "You'll see." What was that? Lama wisdom?

Mark's face softened. He put his hands in his pockets and appeared more relaxed than he had in some time. "Thanks. You know, I always dreamed I'd meet a woman who would be my equal." He spoke quietly, measuring the pace of his words so the meaning sank in. "Someone strong and intelligent, educated, down to earth. The thing about that is," he looked out to sea again, "you never really know if you've met the right person until it happens."

His words swept over and through her, inside and out, leaving her giddy. She was soaring inside, over the top of the tallest mountain with the world spread below. She could not at first find her voice because of the fluttering inside. "I know," she said finally. "I know how that feels."

He turned and looked at her intently. "You do?"

It was too much. "I really should leave you to yourself," she said, changing the subject abruptly.

He looked down at her feet, bare except for the polish on her newly-manicured toes. "You won't get very far without shoes," he said with a grin.

"I was so embarrassed I forgot about them," Kit admitted.

"Don't be," he said, serious again. "Believe me, this was all my fault. You've got nothing to be embarrassed about."

The look he gave her made her wonder if he'd been able to see through her towel,—not possible, but the thought made her cheeks flush anyway. "Listen," she said, clearing her throat. "I really should be going. I can still catch the last flight to New York if I hurry."

"I won't hear of it." Mark stepped toward her, closing the distance between them with all the grace and speed of a tiger. He placed one hand on her arm, gently but firmly, so she could not escape. She felt his warmth through the folds of her clothing, his face just inches above hers in the moonlight.

"If anybody is going to leave tonight, it's me."

That wouldn't work of course. Ruby would be calling later. Kit was certain of it. Mark needed to be here to answer the phone. She got a whiff of his aftershave, woodsy and fresh, the scent she remembered from the day they had met in the cab. "Don't be silly." She looked up, bringing herself dangerously close to his lips. Bad move. "I think the best thing for all concerned is that I leave now."

"Not a chance," Mark said, keeping his grip on her arm. "You won't make that flight to New York in time, and you won't find a hotel room at this hour. It's high season."

He was right.

Mark let go of Kit's arm. She could still feel the warm spot where his hand had been.

"Listen, I know this situation is far from ideal," he began, jangling the change in his pocket again.

Kit couldn't tell whether he meant the situation in which they were stranded alone together, or the situation that he was marrying the wrong woman. Either way, the loose pennies, quarters and dimes in his pockets were getting an Olympic workout.

"I know," he finally said. "Let's make a deal. I'll sleep on the couch, and you can be on your way first thing tomorrow."

The jangling change told Kit he didn't necessarily think it was one of his better ideas. But it made sense. He'd be around to answer the phone when it rang. Kit could fly home and complete her assignment. And nobody would ever know.

"Well," Mark said, "have we got a deal?"

Kit tried to ignore the warning bell that rang madly in the back of her head. *Cling, clang.* She shifted into manual override before giving her answer. "Sure."

Mark's face relaxed. "Good." He pulled his hands from his pockets and shifted toward her, as if he wanted to give her a hug. But then thought better of it. "I have an idea. How about we drive into South Beach and find some dinner?"

"And let all this go to waste?" Kit motioned at the table, hoping to lighten the mood. "I've got a platter of *carne asada* in the kitchen."

He grinned. "Did I hear mention of *carne asada?* Here . . . now?"

"Sí, señor."

"I'll set the table."

They made a good team.

"This is a five-star establishment, Madam," he said in a falsetto whisper, a fair impression of Ethel Van Winterden. "And as my book clearly states, it is always advisable to dine in the best establishment one can possibly afford."

Kit giggled. "Sound advice, Mrs. Van Winterden. I'm glad you approve of our plans for dinner." But in reality, she knew, nothing could be farther from the truth.

A short time later on the balcony, a soft breeze played with a few strands of Kit's hair. "So, have you always been old-fashioned?" She felt comfortable teasing him. Mark had a great sense of humor.

He guffawed. "I wouldn't say that!"

Kit took another forkful of tender meat in a spicy brown sauce. "I think the shoe fits."

Mark watched her chew, letting out a happy sigh. "I wouldn't bet on that. And by the way, excellent choice for dinner. I like a woman who knows her way around *carne asada*."

Kit smiled. "I grew up in Colorado, remember? There's great Tex-Mex there."

Mark nodded with approval. "A lot of people don't like ethnic food."

Kit doubted Ruby ate much besides salad with lemon juice on the side. Always awestruck by tall, slender types who got by on mineral water and field greens Kit had long ago recognized that she was not one of them. She savored another bite of her red beans and rice.

They were dining on the small terrace, under the moonlight, in view of the ocean. The living room, Kit had decided, was off-limits for now. Thanks to her hard work, it screamed boudoir, open and ready for business. Little did Mark know he had been the source of her inspiration. Miami *a deux*, A lovenest for two. That was something he was never going to find out.

She took another sip of wine. "C'mon, Mark, you've got to admit, ten bridesmaids and white limos are not exactly 'thinking outside the box.' It's about as traditional as you can get. Stodgy, even." Kit teased.

He sipped his wine, his eyes warm and luminescent.

The word *dreamboat* came to mind. Kit twirled her glass in one hand, lost in thought, enjoying the view.

The subject was wedding ceremonies, of course. Mark had voiced a preference for a full formal ceremony with all the trimmings, the sort of thing that made most guys groan and make jokes about eloping.

But he was different. Sweet. Sincere. The realization brought on a warm rush inside the silk kimono Kit had changed into for dinner, and spread all the way down to her toes, now encased in slip-on mules topped with tiny matching feather trim. "Stodgy!" she said, trying to hide her true feelings and keep the mood light.

Mark laughed. "Waiter!" He raised one hand in the air to summon imaginary help. "Waiter! Help, I'm getting hammered here."

"If the shoe fits," she said in a singsong voice.

Mark spread his arms wide in mock distress, creating a space big enough to crawl into. He let out a deep sigh of satisfaction, like a release of something that had been building inside him. He leaned back in his chair, studying her with another of his wide trademark smiles. One she hadn't seen for a while.

Kit smiled back. Her feelings of embarrassment about the way he had found her wrapped in a towel had disappeared completely, she realized. In fact, she was laughing and having a lot of fun with him. Mark was easy to be with.

He raised his eyebrows and forced his lips into a pout, throwing the cleft in the center of his chin into bas-relief.

How could one man be so handsome? Kit's breath caught in her throat.

"C'mon," he said, "when you put it like that, I sound like a bore."

"Not at all," Kit put down her wine glass for emphasis. "You're anything but a bore. Do you know how many women would give anything to be sitting here, with you, like this?" She had blurted the words out before she knew what she was saying, and now ducked her head, embarrassed.

She looked back to see him watching her, his eyes narrowed and serious now. It was a reflection of what he saw in her eyes, she knew.

"Thanks," he said quietly.

Kit moistened her lips, embarrassed that she had already said too much. "Well, it's the truth." She meant it. In fact, she couldn't believe it was possible to have this much fun discussing wedding vows with a man who was about to exchange them with someone else—a fact Kit noticed he was careful not to mention.

"Can't we just say I'm a meat and potatoes guy?" Mark took another bite of his *carne asada*.

The way the moonlight fell on the lean lines of his jaw, his high cheekbones made Kit think of how he would look when he was eighty years old. Stunningly handsome no doubt. She shook her head. "Nope. I'm not going to let you off easy."

"C'mon," Mark chuckled. "Well, what about you? You're not exactly cutting-edge yourself."

"I beg to differ." Kit arranged herself primly on her cushions. Mark had set the table using decorations from the living room, right down to cushions for the chairs. He was considerate. Ruby was a lucky girl.

"Anyone who goes for the vow, 'love never fails,' is stodgy in my book."

He remembered. They had discussed Kit's preference for wedding vows at dinner in The Library of The St. Regis.

Mark leaned across the table, close enough to give Kit another delicious whiff of his aftershave. She inhaled deeply, getting a close look at the shadow on his face where his beard had grown since morning. Very sexy.

"Call me what you want," Kit replied. "But, 'love is patient, love is kind,' is your best option. Hands down."

"Really?" Mark frowned, truly interested.

She wondered if he could hear her heart hammering away inside her. She shivered.

He noticed. Time stood still as he reached around her to the velour throw that was draped across the back of her chair.

Their cheeks were almost touching.

Kit felt heat rise from his body in waves that seemed to wash over her. She did not move a muscle as he draped the throw gently around her shoulders, scooping her hair up and out of the way in one smooth motion. His hands lingered near her neck for one or two seconds, but no more. Long enough to make her wonder what it would be like to be married to him.

He settled back in his seat, a bit closer to her than he had been before. His eyes were trained on her. "Warmer now?" He seemed unaware of the effect he had on her.

Kit's insides had turned to something resembling the yolk of a soft-boiled egg. She swallowed hard and nodded, not trusting her voice.

He smiled. "I can't allow Mrs. Van Winterden's number one editor to catch a cold in Miami, can I?"

There was no risk of that. Kit didn't have the nerve to tell him she was not shivering from the cold. She felt a familiar tingling heat up the roots of her hair and spread down to her cheeks. She knew without looking that she had turned thirty shades of hot pink. He could see it, she was certain. The wrap now felt heavy and too warm across her shoulders. She wanted to toss it off, dive into the ocean waves below and swim with him to a secret place in the sea, where it didn't matter that he was engaged to be married.

Mark looked out to sea as if he, too, wished he could find an answer there. The beach was deserted except for the sand shimmering under the silvery light of the full moon.

Kit tried to steer the conversation back to a safe subject. Business was always safe. But in her case, it was weddings. An odd fact, but it was the only thing about which she knew a great deal.

"As I was saying," she said, clearing her throat, "people should stick to the classics when it comes to their weddings." She was on *terra firma* here, thanks to her work at *White Weddings*. "The reading about the different kinds of love is your best bet because between two people there is nothing more important than love. The perfect wedding should be a celebration of that love." Her voice trailed off. Uh-oh, she thought, she sounded like a greeting card. Or worse, like she should be hiking the Himalayas with her mother's ashram.

Mark gave her a look full of admiration, as if she had just announced the discovery of a new DNA sequence. "I've never met anyone who thought so much about different kinds of love."

He had never met her mother's lama. Kit gave him a sharp glance to see if he was teasing.

He appeared to be serious. "Tell me more."

He's not for real, Kit thought. No man would want to discuss this. No man except Edgar, anyway. "What happens at a wedding is so big that words can't really describe it. So your best bet is to keep it short and sweet. I say stick to the classics."

He nodded thoughtfully, considering this. "It's good advice." And then, after a long pause, he added, "If you can manage it."

He was, after all, planning to get married in a ceremony that would be featured in a national magazine, not to mention broadcast live to millions of viewers around the world on morning TV. She saw an image of Ruby, clutching her Blackberry in one perfectly manicured hand and her cell phone in the other. Poor Mark. He would have to beam himself up to Ruby via satellite to get her attention. It was none of Kit's business, she reminded herself. "Trust me," she said, trying to sound breezy. "I'm a professional. I work for a bridal magazine, you know."

A playful look returned to Mark's face. "So," he said, mock serious now, "What is your advice, speaking strictly as a professional?"

Every issue of *White Weddings* included a real-life "Wedding Dos and Don'ts column." It was a favorite among staff and readers alike. The biggest bloopers, she and Edgar had decided long ago, were with couples who wrote their own vows. Edgar was so sure these couples were doomed that he joked that he wanted to follow up with them one year later in a column called "My Big Fat Mean Attorney."

Kit chuckled. "Whatever you do, just don't write your own vows. There's nothing tackier."

Mark winced.

Oops. Ruby was exactly the sort of person who

would want to write her own vows—and force Mark into going along with it, from the look of things. "But it could be a good thing," Kit said, backpedaling quickly. "I mean, I'm sure some bride somewhere decided to read, 'love is patient, love is kind,' at her wedding because it was so original and new." *Thousands of years ago. Nice try.*

Mark slumped a bit lower in his chair.

Kit wanted to lean over, pat him on the shoulder, run her hands along his neck, and make him smile. Feel the warmth of his skin under that shirt. Get him the name of a good attorney. "Reading your own vows makes your wedding truly unique," she said, sounding to her own ears like one of the chapters in Mrs. Van Winterden's book.

Mark glanced out at the ocean again, the look on his face like that of a man who has just been kicked by a rather large horse. Or was beginning to realize he was on the verge of making the biggest mistake of his life.

"Ruby feels the ceremony will be more dramatic if we read our own vows," he said finally.

Kit bit her tongue. She nodded, and gave him what she hoped was an encouraging smile.

Mark sighed. "She's hoping a lot of producers will be watching the ceremony on TV. If it's dramatic enough, it could lead to something."

Kit frowned in spite of her resolve to keep out of it.

"Like a contract to host a talk show of her own," he explained. "She has the idea that she can give people advice on having it all. The perfect wedding, the perfect apartment, the perfect career." He paused and gave a slight shrug. "The perfect life, I guess."

Even if it meant riding roughshod over what her perfect fiancé wanted. Kit fought the urge to harrumph.
She picked up her wine glass and took a sip, forcing
herself to relax her hold so the slender stem wouldn't
shatter into a million pieces. "I see," she said, finally.

Now it was Mark's turn to look sharply at Kit, as
though he did not believe her. "That's her theory anyway," he said, eyes downcast. He looked up, in a visi-
ble effort to lighten the mood. "So, what about *your*
wedding?"

Kit squirmed.

" 'Turnabout is fair play,' " he said with a grin.

For starters, it would include him in a starring role,
she thought. It was a fact she had no intention of shar-
ing with him. "Don't think you can get it out of me by
quoting Shakespeare."

Mark leaned forward. "C'mon. I want to hear all
about the perfect wedding, straight from an editor of
world-famous *White Weddings* magazine, not to mention protégé of Ethel Van Winterden."

Portégé. Little did he know she'd be lucky to have a
job by the time of his wedding. Kit watched him take
another sip of wine, the muscles working in his lean
throat. She felt her stomach lurch, knowing that in one
week's time she'd watch him read his vows to Ruby and
never see him again.

"Come on," he said, playfully. "Tell me what you en-
vision for your wedding day."

It was torture to describe it to him of all people. But
one look at those twinkling brown eyes, inviting and
warm like a sunny day, and Kit knew she couldn't refuse him. The next thing she knew, she was telling him

her dreams about her wedding day. How it would take place inside, not at a clearing in the woods like her father's third wedding. And it would not include chanting the Ohm and a big group hug like her mother's second wedding. Kit would wear a white gown and veil. Nothing over-the-top or lavish enough to make her allergies flare. "I guess it does sound old-fashioned," she said when she was finished.

There was a pause while Kit waited to see if he would tease her. Finally she looked up at him.

He beamed at her. As though he understood everything she had described as well as the dreams of true love she held inside and the way her skin seemed to be humming with electricity under her kimono. "It sounds perfect."

It was too much. Kit looked down and gave a shake of her head, trying to pretend she didn't care so much about him.

He spoke again, his tone low and serious. "You deserve it, Kit."

She glanced up and saw so much admiration in his eyes that she could not hold his gaze. She sniffed. "I'd probably sneeze my way through it."

"Not a chance." Mark shook his head.

"Oh, you don't know my allergies."

"I think I've seen them firsthand," he said with a grin. "But it won't happen on your wedding day, trust me."

"Oh, why's that?"

"Because the groom will keep you from sneezing."

Kit laughed. "Only if I marry an allergy doctor."

Mark shook his head, smiling. "Nope. Any groom will do."

Kit raised an eyebrow.

"I think once you meet the right guy, you'll be fine."

"Well, I guess I haven't got that part worked out yet," Kit admitted. She waited, expecting him to laugh at her. He didn't.

"That part will work itself out." His voice dropped a few octaves. "You just haven't met the right man."

But she had, Kit thought miserably. "Right."

For years Mother had told her the very same thing. So had Edgar. "When you meet the right one it will be like being run over by a ten-ton lorry. Only not as messy," Edgar was fond of saying. He was wrong, though, because this was messy. Mark was already spoken for. A fact Kit needed to accept if she wanted to keep on paying rent, buying food, and doing all the other things a steady paycheck allowed her to do.

Kit looked out at the ocean. The waves were positively dancing in the moonlight. And there was the moon itself, hanging in the sky like a big, ripe peach. A small sigh escaped her lips. *Could this scene be any more romantic?*

And then it was. Mark sang a few lines, something about dancing right up to the stars and far over the waves. His voice was strong and melodious. He was serenading her.

Nobody had ever done that. Kit felt something warm and soft and good start deep down inside and spread throughout her, like heat from the sun on a summer day. She blinked back tears, not trusting herself to speak for a moment. "Bravo," she said finally. "That song is so beautiful. Where'd you learn it?"

Mark smiled. "It's a Dawson family original. My

mother sang it to my brother and me at night on our sailboat. When I was small, I wanted to walk across the waves, reach right up to the moon and grab it."

Kit's eyes misted over, imagining him as a small boy. He must have been all soft brown eyes and chubby little cheeks until that jaw grew in like granite. She thought back to her own childhood on the ranch in Colorado. "On nights when the moon was full like this, I used to think I could climb one of the mountains right up into the sky."

"Growing up in the Rockies must have been wild," Mark said.

Kit nodded but felt a stab of pain at the memory of how it had all come crashing to an end when her parents split up. "My dad used to say we were close to heaven. We lived on a ranch eight thousand feet above sea level."

Mark chuckled, "I'd say your father was right."

Kit smiled. "I had a pony named Pretzel."

"You had a pony?" He leaned forward in mock jealousy. "I always wanted a pony."

"I rode him every day. We had a dog, Sheba, who followed us for miles. I don't recall ever being inside when the sun was shining." She pictured the Aspen trees shimmering in days of endless sunshine.

There was silence as Mark considered this. "You, Ms. McCabe, have led a privileged life."

She nodded. "It didn't last forever. My parents split up. My dad headed to the West Coast. My mother and I moved to New York." She didn't tell him the whole story. How she found herself penned in by skyscrapers and crowds of people, how she cried herself to sleep every night in her tiny room above First Avenue, longing to go back to the home that existed only in her memories.

"That must have been awful for you," Mark said quietly.

"It was," she said abruptly. She had done well at prep school and the elite college she'd attended, throwing herself into her studies. She had shown the same dedication to her career. It was a good way to avoid being hurt.

"You know, Kit, sometimes you can't figure it out on your own. I mean, you think you know exactly how things should go. But you don't know until you find yourself in the situation whether it feels right, whether it feels the way you always hoped it would."

Mark's words brought her attention back to the table, and she sensed he was speaking more for his benefit than for hers.

He was watching her with an expression that was full of kindness. "The only way the hurt will heal is if you take a chance, jump in with both feet and give it a try."

"I suppose," Kit said slowly. What she really thought was that the best thing for her, right now, would be to make a big U-turn and get out of here, before he made her fall any harder for him. Mark Dawson should come equipped with his own private "Enter at Your Own Risk" sign.

"You'll see," he leaned forward, patting her arm.

His touch sent spurts of energy shooting through her like comets racing across the night sky.

"Once you meet the right person, you'll know." He glanced away, out to sea again.

But Kit had seen something in his eyes. A shift. Like he realized something he had not been sure of until now.

"You know, a few months ago I would have argued with you about that," she said.

He looked at her intently. "And now?"

She wanted to tell him she believed he might be right. She wanted him to scoop her up in his arms and hold her until all her fears went away. Kit drew in a shaky breath, stalling for time, before she replied. "Now, I'm not so sure," she said, trying to sound nonchalant.

He nodded, but those warm brown puppy eyes of his had a wounded look. As though this was not the answer he had wanted to hear. As though he cared about her.

Too bad. Kit had work to do. And this conversation was not getting them anywhere. She pushed away her wine glass and stood.

"Guess we'd better clean these up," she said, trying for a brisk tone of voice. She began stacking dishes into a pile.

Mark was on his feet in an instant, his hand brushing against hers as he reached for the plates.

She felt a rush where he touched her. It left her shivering again.

"Not so fast, Cinderella," he said with a smile. "You organized this delicious dinner. I'll do the washing up."

Cinderella. Which made him Prince Charming. A thought Kit needed to ignore under the circumstances, though it was not going to be easy.

Balancing the dishes in one hand, Mark patted the cushion on the back of Kit's chair. "The meal was superb. And the company was intoxicating. "This is the most enjoyable evening I've had since . . . ," he paused, his eyes dark, his tone suddenly serious. "The best night in a long time. Relax and let me do something for you." He put down the dishes and plumped up the cushions on the back of Kit's chair.

She sat still. She wasn't used to being fussed over. It felt good.

Mark collected the plates again. "How about a walk on the beach when I finish up? Maybe a swim before bed?"

Uh-oh. A late-night stroll on the beach with Prince Charming? Under a full moon? "I'm kind of tired," Kit murmured.

Mark looked at her, his eyes narrowing. As though he could read her mind. "Come on, Kit. It will tire us out."

He was right, of course. They had eight hours to get through before dawn. "Okay," she said finally. Even though going for a moonlit stroll on the beach with him made about as much sense as counting money under a Manhattan streetlight in the wee hours. Which is to say, not much sense at all.

But karma doesn't always make sense. It just makes things happen.

Chapter Twelve

*Weddings the Van Winterden Way: Clear up loose ends
well in advance of the wedding day.*

Mark swam hard and fast through the moonlit
waves, which were disappointingly warm. He had
hoped the water would be ice cold, to douse the flames
raging inside him. Just as he had hoped the swim would
tire him out. But he had been doing the freestyle that
had earned him a state ranking in high school, and still
his body was far from spent. In fact, he felt he could
swim all the way to Cuba. The real problem was mental. His mind was racing with thoughts of the gorgeous
woman waiting for him on the beach.

He turned his head and checked the shoreline. Yup.
She was still there, watching him from the water's
edge. Her brow was furrowed with worry.

"There's no lifeguard," she had said when he'd sug-
gested the late-night swim.

She was right of course. "I'll be fine," he'd said through clenched teeth as he took a running start and dove into the dark waves, disregarding everything he had ever learned about water safety. He had swum hard and fast, propelling his body through the waves like a torpedo. The thought of sharks had crossed his mind, but being eaten alive was nothing compared with the feelings that were roiling inside him.

Too late he'd realized it was a mistake to walk on the beach with Kit in the moonlight. She was bright, witty, fun, and easy to be with. And he had caught a glimpse of the black bikini underneath her silk kimono. The kimono was a shade of pale ivory, and set off the emerald color of her eyes in a way that made Mark's heart pump so loud he could hardly hear himself think.

Anything, he had figured, would be better than sitting around the condo, watching the way Kit's face lit up when she smiled (often), listening to the sound of her voice (lyrical), or seeing the way her hair gleamed by candlelight (like copper). He'd had a thing for redheads since the second grade. He had snuck a kiss from Mary Alice O'Toole, and she had slugged him in the nose. He should have learned his lesson then but, of course, he hadn't.

Mark stroked harder, faster, trying not to think of the way it would feel to run his lips over Kit's, and discover if she tasted as sweet as she looked. Just for starters.

He had agreed to a weekend away in part to forget all about Kit, hoping he would feel better about this blasted wedding after a few days away. But then he had walked in and found her exactly where she wasn't supposed to be, invading his thoughts as well as his personal space. Mark took a gulp of air but got seawater instead. He flipped over into survival backstroke and eased himself, sputtering, into the shallows.

Kit raced over. "Are you okay?"

He stood, coughing, and nodded.

She patted his back.

The feel of her hand on his bare skin was like a hundred tiny bolts of lightning, all striking at once, sending a current up and down his spine. Her face was full of concern, while her hand gently rubbed his back.

Mark felt himself lulled by her touch, the gentle motion of the warm waves lapping around his feet, the soft breeze against his bare skin. The way the folds of her kimono lay on her skin in the soft light. He was in the danger zone, and he knew it. He swallowed hard, and his voice was gruff. "I'm fine. Let's walk." It sounded like an order.

Kit looked up at him doubtfully. "Okay. Unless you'd like to take a rest."

"Nope. I'm fine," Mark growled.

"Okay." She looked around at the sky, the ocean, the sand. "It's such a beautiful night." She smiled up at him.

Mark felt his heart melt, and was overpowered by the urge to take her in his arms and kiss her silly, right here and now.

But he knew that Kit wasn't the type of woman to steal a casual kiss. Come to think of it, neither was he. Kissing her would open a door that could never be closed again. It would mean the end of her first big cover story for *White Weddings* magazine and certain disgrace at work, among other things. And he knew from the way she talked that Kit's career meant the world to her. He had a hunch it represented the home she'd lost growing up, the ranch in Aspen, pony and all. It would also spell the end of his plans to marry Ruby. A fact that didn't bother him in the least.

I can't marry Ruby. The realization hit Mark like a lightening bolt, burning deep into his brain and nearly knocking the wind out of him. The sheer force of it pushed a sound from his lips, and along with it, the stress he had felt about the wedding for weeks left him. "Huh."

"Mark? Are you okay?" Kit frowned.

He nodded slowly, calling to mind the way his parents looked at each other even after thirty years of marriage. The way they held hands when they were walking. The way his mother woke up some mornings, her hair mussed, humming while she made his dad breakfast. Happy. The way he knew Kit would look. That settled it.

Mark smiled down at her, feeling the tension wash off him like ocean waves. He fought the urge to throw her in the air and catch her, hold her close to him. "I'm fine. Never better."

She chuckled softly. "That's good to know."

She must have felt the intensity of his gaze, because he saw her cheeks flush. She shivered, tightened the kimono around her and looked down, still smiling. She traced a line in the sand with her toe. "Oh, look!"

The sand glowed and pulsed with silver, sparkling like it had taken on a life of its own. The way his back felt where her soft hand had touched it.

Kit's eyes were round with wonder.

A guy could be happy for the rest of his life to have Kit McCabe look at him like that.

"What is it?"

Mark grinned. "Phosphorescence. It washes in with the tide."

Kit's eyes widened in amazement.

"It's actually millions and millions of creatures so small you'd need a microscope to see them. They wash in on the tide sometimes. You don't see it very often." Mark traced a line in the sand with his toe. The motion left a trail of tiny silver sparks.

Kit clapped her hands. "It's like magic."

Mark felt a lump in his throat. He couldn't take his eyes off her. "Yeah."

She bent down, scooped up a handful of sand and let it trickle through her fingers in a shower of silver sparks. She let out a squeal of delight. "Could this night be any more amazing?"

His entire body tingled with desire. His voice was hoarse with it. "No."

Kit looked up. What she saw in his face made her drop the sand. She rose and stood near him, so that her lips were just inches from his.

Happiness washed over Mark in a powerful wave, leaving a sense of calm in its wake. For the first time in weeks, he felt no doubt or anxiety. He knew what he wanted, and what he needed to do.

Kit must have felt it, too. She tilted her face up to his.

He breathed in her sweet flowery scent, saw the same sense of happiness and wonder on her face that he felt. He did not try to hold back any longer. He reached out and put his arms around her. He gathered her to him, noticing how she felt against him.

Like she was meant to be there.

* * *

Kit felt herself fall.

Mark's arms wrapped around her and pulled her so close she could hear his heart pounding as hard as her own. The waves swirled around their feet, soft and warm.

The inside of Kit's stomach turned to mush. A tide of pleasure coursed through her veins from her toes to the hair on her head. "Ooh." A small coo of pleasure escaped her lips.

Mark gathered her more closely to him.

Her resolve momentarily forgotten, Kit nestled against him and closed her eyes. She could stay this way forever.

"Kit." She heard the rumble of his voice from deep inside his chest. He ran his hands over her back, sending more waves of heat racing through her body.

Kit felt his lips brush the top of her head. Instinctively, she raised her face toward his and opened her eyes.

The light of the moon threw his face into shadow, silhouetting his chiseled cheekbones and jaw. His eyes looked endlessly deep.

The world seemed to stop turning as Kit waited for the touch of Mark's lips on hers. She had been waiting her entire life for this moment, a fact she had not admitted to herself until now. She moistened her lips with her tongue, held her mouth close to his. She saw wonder in his eyes as he gazed down at her.

"Kit," he said again with a tiny shake of his head, holding her even tighter against him as though he just wanted to say her name again. "What are we doing here, on this beach, just the two of us?"

Kit tried to speak but didn't trust her voice.

Mark spoke, each word adding to the waves of pure pleasure that were running through Kit. "I know I should be here with Ruby, but being here with you just seems so right."

Each word filled Kit with wonder. She had always wanted someone speak to her like this, and now it was happening. She felt her spirit soar.

Mark's eyes were darker than ever, filled with sweetness and something else. His next words were simple and direct. "Kit, I'm falling for you. I've never felt this way."

In that moment Kit felt as though she had been in love with him forever. She knew with a certainty she hadn't dared admit to herself that he had all the qualities she had ever wanted in a man. She longed to tell him how she felt, to share her feelings with him. But she didn't dare. She straightened up, almost imperceptibly. She didn't trust her feelings.

But Mark kept her firmly in his grasp, his eyes still loving and warm, and he smiled. "It doesn't make any sense, does it?"

Kit nodded. There was so much she wanted to tell him. She drew in a deep breath, not sure of what to say or where to begin.

A wave lapped around their ankles.

The muscles in Mark's jaw were moving fast, furious. He stared deep into her eyes. A frown played around his forehead. "Let's get you back inside," he said with a small sigh, in a voice that was tender and sweet. It was a tone she had not heard him use before, not even with Ruby.

His arms released her, but seemed to shake with the effort. "It's late," he said softly. "It's been a long day. And, we can't . . ." His voice trailed off.

Kit allowed herself to be led gently back across the silvery sand to the condo. Mark held her hand. She could have walked a million miles like that, feeling his hand around hers.

When they reached the condo, Mark led Kit onto the balcony again and poured each of them another glass of wine. He handed a glass to her wordlessly and watched her take a sip. Their eyes met in a silent toast.

Kit looked out over the ocean. She felt the entire situation wasn't real. She looked up at the moon, perfect and full, glowing in a cloudless sky. The stars were shining so bright she felt she could reach out and grab one, like in the dream she had as a little girl. The thought brought tears to her eyes. Kit knew what her wish would be. That this night would never end.

The thought of tomorrow, and what it would bring, sent a chill through her. She shivered and hugged herself for comfort.

Beside her, Mark saw it. He reached over and took her wine glass from her hand, and quickly set both their glasses down on the table behind them. He scooped Kit into his arms.

The thrill of his arms around her again was too much. She felt like she was home. She could not fight her feelings any longer. "Mark," she whispered.

He opened his mouth to speak but all that came out was her name. "Kit." His voice was deep with emotion. He pulled her closer.

Kit realized that this is how it was supposed to be. She turned her face and waited for his kiss.

Mark brought his lips to hers in a gentle, sweet, soft kiss.

Kit allowed herself to lean into his arms, feeling herself let go and relax. She forgot all about the facts that he was engaged to marry somebody else, and was poison for her career. She knew she would get hurt but she could not fight it any longer. *Mark.* Her mind filled with him.

A thrill of excitement ran up and down Kit's spine. Her eyes fluttered open with pleasure, taking in the silvery moonlight and the warm, soft night air that surrounded them.

She wanted the moment to last forever.

And then his cell phone rang.

Chapter Thirteen

Weddings, the Van Winterden Way: Myth or reality? Is it bad luck to see the bride in her gown before the big day?

Kit stiffened and pulled away.

Mark was very still, his eyes screwed shut.

The cell phone continued to ring shrill and insistent.

He opened his eyes and looked sadly at her, then shook his head.

Kit shivered.

Mark hurried inside and answered the phone.

Kit stared out at the beach, feeling her spirits plummet. For a brief moment, she had felt the night was magical, and anything was possible. Now that feeling was lost. The moon was lower, turning the waves the color of old putty now. A breeze had picked up, sending a chill through the air. Kit hugged herself, remembering the only reason she'd met Mark Dawson was to write a story about his wedding.

She tried to shut out the low rumble of his voice from inside the living room.

"Sweet Pea no, no," came drifting out.

It was Ruby on the other end of the phone. Ruby, who had called to tell her fiancé about her day, never suspecting that when the phone rang his arms would be wrapped firmly around another woman. Kit winced. She was now officially the other woman. The words grew until they filled her mind, pushing away every other thought. *Other woman.*

No, Kit thought. *Never.* She swept her hair behind one ear with her hand, as though she could erase the touch of his lips. She wanted Mark, but not like this. No man was worth it.

Kit shivered again and turned away from the ocean. It was now dark and cold. She tried to stop shivering but could not. She ached inside. But it was nothing, she knew, compared with the ache she would feel if she gave herself to Mark without receiving anything in return.

She stepped softly inside.

Mark sat on the edge of the couch, hunched over his cell phone. The expression on his face was pained. He looked up as she entered, and half rose off the couch.

Kit raised her hand to stop him.

Frowning, he pulled the phone away from his ear. He looked at her, his jaw set into a tight, hard line.

From the receiver came the tinny sound of a voice on the other end of the connection.

Kit shrugged, giving a small wave of her hand.

Mark looked down, took a deep breath, and put the phone back to his ear. "Yeah," he said, "I'm still here."

Kit walked into the bedroom and shut the door behind her. She leaned against it and tried not to cry. She folded her arms across her chest to stop the shaking that rocked her body.

For one brief, fleeting moment she had experienced what it would be like to have it all, perfect love from a perfect man. She had gotten a sense of how it would feel. *Home.* That was the only word she could use to describe it.

But it wasn't real, she reminded herself. All Mark Dawson had to offer was a single night of passion. Stolen from someone else.

Kit sniffed loudly. She should be happy to have avoided that, she told herself. She shrugged off the kimono and threw on her nightgown. She headed into the bathroom and brushed her teeth.

She climbed into bed and switched off the light. But her lips were still full of Mark's kisses, her insides still warm from the memory of his touch. She wished more than anything that he would open the bedroom door and tell her he realized he was about to make the biggest mistake of his life. That he wanted to be with her, not Ruby.

But it didn't happen. Kit tossed and turned on the satin sheets, rolling from one side of the bed to the other until it seemed the size of a postage stamp.

She finally gave up, reached for the clicker, and switched on the Lattingly's giant, state-of-the-art forty-two-inch plasma television.

She surfed through channels. Until a familiar face filled the screen, up close and larger than life. Kit felt the hair rise on the back of her neck.

The voice of Mrs. Ethel Van Winterden floated through the stereo speakers, and filled the room.

"Any woman can have the wedding of her dreams, as shown in my new book, *Rules of Engagement*." Great White hoisted a book the size of the Manhattan white pages in one tiny manicured hand, as though it was as light as a feather.

Kit shuddered.

The image changed as the camera moved in for a close-up of Ruby Lattingly, who flashed a dazzling white smile.

The sight took Kit's breath away.

Ruby wore a crown on top of her head. A tiara. Sparkling and dancing in the light, as though she was born to wear it.

Kit swallowed painfully.

A group of men, armed with straight pins and scissors, were gathered around Ruby like the Swiss Guard attending to European royalty. They applauded happily as the camera pulled back to reveal Ruby's gown. Gleaming white and gossamer thin with two tiny spaghetti straps. It looked, Kit thought, as though it had been sewn on. All the better to show off Ruby's impossibly thin figure.

Kit realized she was watching a taping of Ruby's bridal gown fitting earlier in the day. It must have been the reason she had not traveled to Miami with Mark.

On screen, Ruby giggled, "I hope my fiancé's not watching this. I don't want him to see what I'm doing while he's out of town."

And Mark would feel the same about what he was doing, Kit thought bitterly.

Ruby's tiara sparkled on screen. "I've always wanted to be a princess on my wedding day."

"And now you will be," Great White answered, like some demented version of Good Witch Glenda. She turned slowly to the camera and smiled, revealing a mouth crowded with tiny, razor-sharp teeth.

Kit pulled the covers up around her chin, pushing as far back against the pillows as she could. She knew any sane person would hit the clicker and switch the thing off, but she couldn't bring herself to do so.

"Planning a wedding is simple with the help of my new book," Great White continued.

The camera panned the book and its cover, then Ruby in her tiara. And finally, one last look at Great White with her beady black eyes that seemed to bore holes directly into Kit's skull from the TV.

Kit shuddered and switched the clicker off, throwing the room into darkness.

Ruby did indeed have it all. While Kit had nothing more than kisses stolen from Ruby's man. Kit knew she had done the right thing. But it didn't change the fact that it hurt. A tear rolled down her cheek in the darkness, then another and another.

Kit let them fall until they made the pillow damp. She reached out in the darkness to grab a tissue from her pocketbook. She reached inside and knew right away what she found. A white linen handkerchief with the letter *D* embroidered on one corner in blue thread. It unleashed a torrent of hot, salty tears.

Kit had, for the first time, dared to believe she had finally met the man of her dreams. She had opened herself up to him, if only for a moment. Heart and soul. Mark Dawson had come into her life and unlocked something deep inside her. But she knew he was not meant to be hers. Kit could not understand why she had been given a taste of love if it wasn't meant to be. Maybe karma was like that.

Kit was high on the mountain, riding her pony through the trees. Her father's ranch was as she had remembered it. She was happy. The sun was shining. The pony trotted along until they came to a small stream. Mark Dawson stood on the other side. He called out to her, beckoning her to come to him.

The pony balked. Kit dismounted and walked to the water's edge. She looked across at Mark.

He was mouthing words but no sound came. He motioned with his hand for her to cross.

She needed to find a way across the stream. There were some stepping stones but they were covered in moss, slippery, and wet.

Mark stepped closer to the edge of the stream and motioned again for Kit to cross.

She was afraid, but she wanted—needed—to get to him. Kit stepped out onto the first rock. And found herself falling . . .

She landed in a sea of white tulle. She was a contestant on a game show called *Win That Groom*, dressed in a wedding gown, and locked in a battle of wits with a crowd of other brides. They all wore white tulle. The winner would go home with Mark Dawson.

He stood alone on top of a giant wedding cake, his arms stretched out to Kit. "Win me," he mouthed the words, "win me."

Kit tried to come up with the right answer, but she couldn't force the words out of her mouth.

Mark reached out, beckoning her. Kit tried to reach him. She found herself in a long, dark hallway, running to him. But the dress got in her way, holding her back. She felt herself sinking into something like quicksand.

A bell rang. Time was running out. A judge cloaked in heavy black robes appeared and shook her head. "Wrong answer."

Kit recognized the tiny robed outline of Ethel Van Winterden. She shuddered.

Great White rang the bell again. "Time's up."

"No" Kit yelled. She leaned forward, trying to reach Mark but the dress weighed her down. She strained, trying to run. Her legs would not move.

Great White came closer. There were no eyes inside those trademark tortoiseshell eyeglasses. Just empty black holes.

Kit screamed.

Great White smiled, revealing a double row of gleaming white teeth. She hit the bell again. "Out of time."

Kit moaned.

The bell rang again.

Kit woke up.

It had only been a dream.

Relief flooded through her, along with something else. Kit tried desperately to remember the dream. She was certain there was something she needed to know. But the image escaped her. She had the vague feeling she had been back in Colorado at her childhood home, but none of it was real.

A telephone rang. That part of the dream was real.

Bright sunlight spilled through the blinds. Kit remembered where she was. Mark's voice, deeply serious, rumbled through the door. Kit dropped her head back onto the pillow and closed her eyes. She wished she could go back to sleep. Back to her dream.

A quick rap sounded on the door. Without waiting for an answer, Mark walked in. There were hollows under his eyes. Kit realized he had not slept any more than she had. And a dark stubble of beard on his jaw. Very attractive, she thought.

Kit sat up.

His gaze softened as it found Kit, coming to rest on the jumble of red hair on her shoulders. His mouth softened. "Good morning. I'm sorry to barge in."

He stood at the foot of the bed. If he had waited all night to tell her he was in love with her, he was off on the wrong foot. He looked as jittery as a horse that had just seen a snake slide across its path.

Mark ran a hand through his hair. "That was Ruby on the phone."

His words added more weight to the heavy feeling in the pit of Kit's stomach. He obviously wasn't going to grab her in his arms and give her a passionate kiss.

Instead, he crossed them in front of his chest, shifting his weight from one foot to the other. He cleared his throat. "She's downstairs. In the parking lot."

"What?" Kit sat bolt upright, clutching the blankets up to her chin.

"She caught the early flight from New York." Mark surveyed the room in a quick inventory, his gaze coming to rest on Kit's overnight bag. "Things went better than she thought. She decided to come down early and surprise me."

A flash of sheer terror went through Kit, turning her limbs to ice.

Mark shifted his weight once more.

From the living room there was the sound of the front door opening, straining against the chain.

"Yikes." Kit's voice came out in a squeak. She froze in place, too terrified to move.

Fingernails tapped on the front door in three short bursts. Long, red fingernails. Like talons. Kit remembered them.

She shuddered, slid off the bed, and scanned the room for any possible means of escape. All she came up with was the window. Too high.

Mark reached out and took Kit by the arm.

It made her heart start pounding, fluttering inside her chest like a bird beating its wings against a cage.

"Everything will be okay," he said in a low voice.

Fingernails rapped again on the front door, sending ripples of fear through Kit's veins.

"Yoo-hoo," Ruby called. "Darling, it's me. Why do you have the chain on the door? Open up."

Mark tightened his grip on Kit's arm, his voice low and urgent. "I'll take her for a walk on the beach while you . . ." He glanced again at Kit's suitcase.

"Right," Kit whispered. Walks on the beach were getting to be Mark's specialty, she thought with a pang of bitterness. She wanted to get out of here fast.

She was about to make a beeline to the closet and her traveling pantsuit when Mark pulled her close to him.

Kit looked into his eyes. Bad move. She felt heat again in the pit of her stomach. In no time, it seeped through her, making her flush.

His gaze was soft, beseeching. "Kit," he whispered.

Ruby's voice came through the door again, more insistent. "Darling, it's me. Open up."

Kit stared at Mark and somehow found the will to remove her arm from his hold. *So this is what it was like to be the other woman.*

A shadow passed over his face. He shook his head sadly. "I don't want things to be this way."

Kit nodded sadly as Ruby's voice, louder now, called out again from the door.

Mark's jaw worked furiously, as though there was something he wanted to say, but it was too late for conversation.

Kit raced into the bathroom and shrugged off her nightgown. She needed to get out.

Mark left the bedroom, closing the door behind him.

Kit pulled on her pantsuit as quietly as she could and gathered her things. She tiptoed to the door and listened to the sounds of their reunion in the living room.

"I love what you've done with the place." Ruby squealed with delight.

Kit heard their footsteps walking through the condo. Ruby remarked on various accent pieces that Kit had chosen with care.

The sound of footsteps approaching the bedroom door made Kit stand as still as a statue.

Ruby's voice was pitched high with happiness. "Darling, I can't believe you did all this for me. You are the most thoughtful . . . ," she paused, and there was a loud smooching sound. "Most sensitive . . ." Another kiss. "Most romantic fiancé in the entire world."

Ugh. A churning sensation, like mud being stirred in slow motion, was tearing up the inside of Kit's stomach.

Mark's voice was quiet, tight. "Don't make too much of it."

Kit squeezed her eyes shut and prayed they would leave before she had to hear any more.

"You must have worked all day on this," Ruby exclaimed.

Six hours to be precise.

Ruby's next words made Kit's blood turn cold.

"I can't wait to see what you've done in the bedroom."

Kit held her breath.

"No. Later," Mark said firmly.

"Come on," Ruby said, playful now. "I want a personal tour."

Kit stared at the doorknob, praying it wouldn't move. Her heart pounded so hard against her ribs she was certain they could hear it.

"No, Sweet Pea." Mark's voice was tighter now, very tense. "You can see it later. Let's go for a walk on the beach."

Ruby's voice dropped a notch, still playful, teasing. "Come on, darling, take me to the budoir."

Kit was not sure if she would faint or vomit.

There was a rustling sound outside the bedroom door.

Kit stared at the doorknob, her ears filled with the roar of her own blood. If the handle moved, all was lost.

"No, Ruby." Mark's voice was forceful now. "I said no. Not now."

More rustling noises, too close for comfort.

"Come on," Ruby's voice was singsong now, and coy. "You know you want to show me what you've done with the place."

The churning in Kit's stomach grew stronger until she felt it would implode. She no longer cared if she was discovered.

"No. Not now." Mark's voice had a metallic edge to it. "Beach first."

Kit stood stock still, not daring even to back away from the door for fear of hitting a loose floor board. *Please,* she prayed silently, *please make them go away.*

"Okay." Ruby finally backed down. "Beach first. We've got the rest of our lives, after all."

Kit grimaced, certain she was about to throw up.

Just as she drew in a breath of relief, the doorknob rattled.

Ruby wasn't giving up.

"I'll just slip inside and change into my suit." Ruby's voice floated through the door, closer than ever now.

Kit was shaking so hard her teeth began to chatter. She snapped her mouth shut so they wouldn't hear.

"Not so fast." Mark's voice was loud now.

"Mark, what are you . . ." Ruby squealed in surprise, and there was the sound of more movement.

The doorknob shook one more time as Ruby's hand slid off.

Kit stared at it as though it was possessed.

Mark's voice dropped, quiet now. He was changing tactics. "We'll go to the beach if I have to carry you all the way out there."

There was silence. Then more kissing sounds.

Kit's felt her heart shatter into a million pieces, each digging into the lining of her stomach.

"A bride could get used to this," Ruby's voice, muffled now, grew fainter with the sound of heavy footsteps moving down the hall.

Kit covered her mouth with both hands and took a deep breath. A sob caught in her throat. She pressed hard and stifled the sound.

A few moments later the front door finally closed behind them, as the future Mr. and Mrs. Mark Dawson headed out for a romantic stroll on the beach. Miami *à deux*.

Kit grabbed her gear. She ducked her head onto the balcony. She couldn't resist one last look.

They were easy to spot, strolling down the beach hand in hand. Gotham's most in-love couple. At least the day had not turned into Miami *à trois*.

Chapter Fourteen

Weddings, the Van Winterden Way: An experienced wedding planner can smooth over last-minute surprises or changes of plan.

Kit's flight back to New York passed in a numb haze. She felt dull, flattened, too sad even to cry. If she started, she was afraid she'd never stop. No matter how much she tried, she could not rid herself of the sound of Mark carrying Ruby off down the hall.

It did not change the fact that her lips ached where his had touched them, or the memory of how his arms felt wrapped around her, or the twinkle she remembered in his eyes when he looked at her. The truth was, Kit had fallen for Mark Dawson. Hard.

She headed straight to the office, determined to lose herself in work. She labored over the "Rough Cuts" piece all afternoon and into early evening, ignoring the phone when it rang. Nobody would expect the phone at *White Weddings* to be answered on a Sunday afternoon.

Each photo of twinkling candles or soft pillows reminded Kit of the love she had hoped for but not found.

Darkness had settled on the streets by the time she finished. She walked a copy upstairs to Mrs. Van Winterden's office and left another for Edgar to review. At least she had turned in the assignment on time. At least she might keep her job.

She took a cab across town, stopping at her favorite takeout place, Sushi à Go-Go. She ate her dinner in front of the television. The phone rang but she ignored it. Both Edgar and her mother knew she was in Miami, and everyone else could leave a message.

She went to bed without even bothering to unpack, and fell into a deep sleep.

Mark couldn't sit still. He felt like a tiger in a cage. He had been trapped inside the *White Weddings* conference room for most of the morning. What he really wanted was to run through the halls in search of Kit, take her in his arms, and say to her all the things he should have said in Miami.

He shook his head in disbelief when he thought of the events of the last forty-eight hours. He paced to the window and looked out. From here, it was impossible to see the sidewalk below. But he knew the press was down there, waiting for him with cameras, microphones, and spotlights. Or worse, they were waiting for Kit. The thought of her squeezed his heart until it ached. He needed to find her. Now.

The sound of Mrs. Van Winterden's voice, low and breathy, made him turn his head. She gave a small smile, all business, and motioned to the empty seat at the conference table. "Almost done."

Mark took his seat again wordlessly, aware that the assorted members of *White Weddings* marketing, public relations and legal teams were trying not to stare. He'd spent the last hour and a half explaining the details of his breakup with Ruby to them. Everything except why. Mark ran a hand through his hair, and tried to focus on the documents in front of him, but all he could think of was finding Kit.

"This states that you are responsible for specific non-reimbursed expenses associated with the wedding."

Mark gave her a quizzical glance.

Mrs. Van Winterden cleared her throat. "Basically, the ring from Tiffany should Miss Lattingly refuse to return it."

"Where do I sign?" Mark said savagely, his pen poised. He wanted to find Kit so badly his legs twitched from the effort of sitting still. His breakup with Ruby on the beach yesterday had been fast, faster than he had expected. Ruby, it turned out, was in as much of a hurry to get back to New York City as he was. Her agent had been planning a Monday morning press conference anyway.

Mark had raced to Miami Airport, but by then Kit's flight had gone. He caught the next one, and spent most of the day and a good part of the evening trying to track her down. But it was no use. He'd hung around the *White Weddings* offices until the security guard threatened to call the police, and finally resorted to walking the streets where they'd first met in the cab. Still no Kit. He had spent another sleepless night.

Mrs. Van Winterden spoke, bringing him back to earth. "Last one," she said. "This one states that you agree not to enter any future contests sponsored by *White Weddings* magazine or its affiliates."

There was a general shuffling of papers, tapping of pens, and perhaps even a muffled snicker among the crowd across the table. Mark signed the document quickly, anxious to leave.

"Well done." Mrs. Van Winterden stood, signaling the meeting was finally over.

The staff began filing out, murmuring good-byes.

Nobody stopped to shake Mark's hand. "I'd like just one more minute of your time," he said when he was alone with Mrs. Van Winterden.

She glanced at her watch, then at him, tiny eyebrows raised above the line of her trademark tortoiseshell frames.

"First, thank you for all the work you've done on the wedding."

The founding editor nodded.

"And I am sorry about how things turned out," he continued, shoving his hands in his pockets. He felt like an idiot. No Dawson man, he knew, had ever left his bride at the altar.

The room was so quiet Mark could hear the droning of a helicopter over the Hudson.

"It's over now, Mr. Dawson," Mrs. Van Winterden replied evenly. "No need to worry. We are professionals."

She was called the wedding diva for good reason,

Mark thought. Ruby's stunt this morning had, however, caught them both off guard.

She had held a press conference on the steps of the Mid-Manhattan Church to announce the end of her engagement to Mark Dawson and the cancellation of her fabulous, over-the-top, *White Weddings*-sponsored nuptial bash. She also took the opportunity to announce she would be hosting a new reality show on cable TV, *Relationship 911,* offering advice to couples on the rocks. The first episode would feature a jilted bride whose fiancé had been caught with another woman.

The press had had a field day with it. One local news show quickly revived the previous week's *New York Post* photo of Kit smiling at Mark, glowing with love which they had run over the caption, "His Cheatin' Heart." Mark winced at the memory.

Two photographers had waylaid him that morning, and several more were waiting outside the *White Weddings* offices when he arrived. Hopefully Kit had not met the same fate.

Kit. He needed to tell her he was free. He wanted to hold her in his arms again, to breathe in her delicious scent, taste her lips, and pick up where they had left off. Mark was finished with keeping up appearances. He knew what he wanted now—Kit. But first he had to find her. And at the moment the steely-eyed Ethel Van Winterden was his best bet.

"I wish you the best in your future endeavors, Mr. Dawson." The founding editor turned to go. "If you'll excuse me, I've got a number of editorial pages to fill."

"I just need a minute. Please." Mark refused to leave. He could tell by the look on her face she was not accustomed to being disobeyed.

She looked at him, her eyes narrowing behind her thick lenses.

Mark felt the room grow warm around him. The air felt close, as if it lacked oxygen. His collar felt too tight. He ran a hand around it, tugging at it. He needed to make this woman understand that Kit had had nothing to do with anything that had happened. Nothing.

"I don't know how to say this, so I'm just going to tell you the truth," he began. "I didn't know what real love felt like till the day I met Kit McCabe."

Mrs. Van Winterden pursed her tiny lips in a clear sign that this was more, much more, information than she needed.

"I had realized marrying Ruby was a mistake. Frankly, I had known all along, on some level, that I needed to end it. And so I did. But none of this had anything to do with Kit. Trust me on that." He looked at the older woman. Her face was impossible to read.

"Kit was only trying to do her job," Mark said. "She worked hard on this, and she's wonderful at her job. In fact, she's just plain wonderful." His voice cracked, to his horror. He swallowed hard and continued anyway. "And I need to get in touch with her. Right away."

A small, tight smile appeared on Mrs. Van Winterden's lips. "I appreciate your candor, Mr. Dawson, and I wish you all the best. And now, if you'll excuse me,

I've got a lot of press calls to return." She turned to go—meaning they were finished.

Frustration rose up and engulfed Mark like a wave. Kit was slipping away from him, and her career was slipping away from her—right before his eyes. It wasn't fair. He spoke again, his voice low and urgent. "Haven't you ever realized you needed to make a change?"

Mrs. Van Winterden turned to face him again, surveying him coolly. "You're asking if I've made mistakes? Of course I have. I built this magazine into the best in the industry by recognizing my mistakes. When I see one, I fix it. Immediately."

Her tone was dismissive, and her words left no doubt that she intended to correct a mistake or two immediately—Including one named Kit McCabe.

"I'm not talking about mistakes," Mark said evenly. "I'm talking about change. How one day you think you have everything figured out. And the next you learn something new. And then nothing is ever the same again. You need to change. It's not a mistake. It's just life." He thought of Kit's word to him in the cab on the day they met. *Karma.*

Then something remarkable happened. Mark witnessed a surprising change in the founding editor's face. One moment, she looked away, lost in thought. The next, her face softened. It might have been just reflection of light in her signature lenses. But perhaps Ethel Van Winterden, the tiny woman with the big reputation for making lovers' dreams come true, had gotten in touch with some karma of her own. "What you do with your life now is your own business, Mr. Dawson. I hope you manage to keep it out of the tabloids, for your sake." She turned to go.

"But if you must know, you will find Kit McCabe at City Hall in one hour."

Across town, Kit had been dreaming again. This time, she had chased Mark down a long hallway with polished floors and fluorescent lights. But the tulle kept getting in her way.

The sound of a ringing phone woke her.

She awoke, grateful to be in her own bed. Then she remembered. It was one day closer to Mark's wedding. Her heart sank. She could tell by the uneasy feeling she had that she had had the dream again. There was something Kit desperately needed to do. She was certain of it. But what?

The phone continued to ring and she glanced at the clock before answering. She had overslept. She glanced at caller ID. *White Weddings*. She groaned aloud and picked up.

It was Mrs. Van Winterden's assistant, asking if Kit could come to the office—right away—to review her work.

Kit replied she would be there in half an hour.

She raced through the shower, dressing yet again in her classic navy blue suit and pumps. She had a feeling she was going to need to make as good an impression as possible. She swept her hair back with the tortoiseshell clip Edgar had given her for good luck, and applied her makeup and lip gloss with care before running out the door.

Hailing a cab was a cinch at mid-morning. Kit settled into the back seat and hit speed-dial for Edgar at work. He answered on the first ring.

"It's me."

Edgar chuckled, "How are things at home? Inquiring minds want to know."

"I overslept, that's all."

"I can see why. Details to follow, I hope. Are you alone? Or can't you say?"

"I can say." Kit frowned but chose to ignore the comment, deciding Edgar obviously enjoyed the fantasy that she had invited Mark to join her in Miami. She checked the nearest street sign. "I'm in a cab on Fifty-third, just about to cross Fifth. On my way to a meeting with Great White."

"Uh-oh," Edgar's tone grew serious. "I'm sorry, Cookie."

Tiny tingles of nervous energy made the hair stand up on the back of Kit's neck. "She wants to go over my 'Rough Cuts' piece. I didn't think condolences were in order. Have you looked at it? Is it okay?"

"It's fine. No problem," Edgar began.

Relief flooded through Kit. At least *that* wouldn't be on the founding editor's agenda.

"In fact, I'd try to focus on that," Edgar said.

The tone of his voice set off alarm bells. "As opposed to what?"

Edgar sounded incredulous. "You've really been sleeping all morning?"

Kit shrugged. "Yeah."

He sighed, "Oh, Cookie, I've been trying to call you since dawn. Have you turned on the telly today?"

Kit straightened up with a sense of alarm. "No. Should I have?" Somehow she already knew the answer to that question.

"Where are you now?"

The tone of Edgar's voice had shifted from alarm to full-scale red alert. "At the corner of Sixth. Close to the office. What's the matter?"

But it was too late. Kit could see the problem.

A group of men and women crowded the sidewalk outside *White Weddings'* offices. Cameras were slung around their necks.

Kit wanted to order the driver to keep going, but it was too late. He had already pulled up to the curb. And she had been spotted.

A shout went up among the paparazzi. They stampeded to her cab, cameras trained on her.

Kit felt her knees turn to rubber. She fumbled for her wallet and paid the driver with shaking hands, while flashes popped all around her like a Rocky Mountain lightning storm in August.

Edgar tried to help with advice over the phone. "If you've got dark glasses, put them on!"

It was far too late for that. Kit pushed the cab door open and took a shaky step onto the curb. Directly into the crowd of paparazzi. She pushed through as best she could. The shouting was frightening.

"Kit, Kit!" one of them called.

Kit looked over. Bad move. A camera was pushed into her face. A flash popped.

"Do you have a boyfriend?"

"Were you responsible for Mark and Ruby's breakup?"

"Has he asked you to marry him?"

"What do you think of Ruby's new cable show?"

"Do you still have a job?"

"Are you in love with Mark Dawson?"

Kit's ears burned, her heart pounded, and the inside of her mouth was so dry her tongue stuck to it. Not surprisingly, the corners of her mouth turned down. She fought back sobs while the cameras whizzed. She hoisted her briefcase in the air and used it as a battering ram to clear a path to the revolving door.

Edgar was waiting just inside. "Poor thing." He ushered her through the lobby to the guard desk.

For once, Kit was grateful for the building's tight security.

The guard gave her a sympathetic nod when she flashed her ID.

Edgar's words didn't soothe the panic Kit felt. "The big boss is waiting. Head straight up," he said, motioning to the express car. Edgar steered Kit onboard.

The doors slid shut behind them. The penthouse button was pre-lit. Kit felt trapped. The car began to rise with a whoosh. They did not have much time. "What's going on?"

Edgar patted her shoulder. "Chin up. It's bad."

"How bad?" Kit demanded.

"Is that mascara waterproof?"

Kit groaned.

The floors were whizzing past.

"Talk fast," Kit ordered.

"Gotham's most in-love couple is no more."

Kit's heart leaped. This was promising news.

Her hopes were, however, dashed by Edgar's next

words. "But it was messy. Blondie held a press conference to announce the breakup. High drama."

Kit's eyes widened in disbelief.

"My mole in P.R. tells me their phones have been ringing off the hook."

Which meant the publicity campaign for Mrs. Van Winterden's new book was in tatters. Kit's heart dropped even further.

Edgar's brow was furrowed in sympathy. "She's on the warpath."

Kit sighed. "Do you have any good news?"

One look at her friend's face told her he did not. Edgar took a deep breath. "Blondie fingered you in the breakup."

"What?" Kit reeled dizzily as Edgar's words sunk in. The breath left her lungs all at once, leaving her ears ringing. "That's not fair," Kit stammered. "I didn't . . . I mean, we didn't . . . ," Her voice trailed off as the doors slid open on the hushed hallway of the publisher's suite. "Is Mark . . . ?"

Edgar gave a quick shake of his head. "No sign of him."

Kit looked down, her eyes wet with tears. Mark had broken up with Ruby, leaving Kit to face the heat. Kit was fairly certain the pain she felt inside her suit jacket was the result of her heart breaking.

"Chin up, Cookie. None of that." Edgar gave her shoulder a final squeeze, and slid a tissue up Kit's sleeve. "Remember, your 'Rough Cuts' piece was fab. I mean it."

Maybe it would help her find another job—somewhere in South America where nobody knew her.

Edgar gave her a small push off the elevator and blew a kiss.

"I'll come to your office when it's over," Kit said over her shoulder.

Edgar shook his head. "Sorry, luv. I'm headed downtown. Last-minute assignment. I'll call as soon as I can."

Kit nodded miserably. Last-minute assignment. All of her colleagues would need to work frantically now, because of the hole in the lineup where Kit's cover story was supposed to be. She blinked back tears.

Mrs. Van Winterden's assistant waved Kit inside cheerily. Kit noticed the woman had been careful to avoid meeting her gaze.

Kit entered Great White's lair, feeling like a hunted baby seal.

"Ms. McCabe. Sit down." Mrs. Van Winterden swung around from her desk. She collected a pile of documents and tapped them several times against the gleaming mahogany to straighten them, then clasped her hands on top.

Kit sank low into the guest chair wordlessly.

"I won't waste time reviewing the events of this morning, as I've got a busy day ahead. And I take it you're fully aware of the situation." Great White watched Kit, in the manner of a fisherman who has hauled up something foreign in his net. Kit nodded. Her instincts told her the best approach would be to say nothing and get this over with as quickly as possible.

"I've reviewed the piece you turned in for *The Feathered Nest.*"

Kit held her breath, waiting to see if her work had passed muster.

"It was adequate," Great White continued.

Kit wasn't sure she'd heard correctly.

"For a first effort. Which is good news for you." The founding editor looked down at the sheaf of papers on her desk. "Because frankly, Ms. McCabe, you have bigger problems than that."

And that was only half the story. The small balloon of happiness that had started to float skyward inside Kit burst. She felt heat rise through her neck to her cheeks and ears. She nodded, eyes downcast. She was about to be fired and she knew it.

Great White cleared her throat.

Here it comes, Kit thought.

"I came close to terminating your employment this morning." Great White's eyes glittered behind her glasses.

Kit flinched.

"But to do so would only excite the media further, which wouldn't be in the best interests of the magazine at this time."

Kit waited wordlessly, still not daring to speak.

"So, I'll keep you on board for now."

It took a minute for Great White's words to work their way through Kit's shocked brain. As their meaning sunk in, Kit's eyes widened in pure surprise. She hadn't expected to keep her job, especially after seeing the pack of paparazzi outside. Slowly, she realized she should say something. "Thank you," she murmured in a voice that was not at all steady.

Great White waved her hand. "No thanks are necessary. I'm just acting in the best interests of this magazine."

Kit's cheeks stung as though she had been slapped.

The founding editor leaned forward. "I am assigning you to a new story. We have a number of pages to fill now that we have lost the Lattingly-Dawson wedding. You'll have a tight deadline."

Kit nodded. "Fine. No problem." She opened her notebook and reached for her pen, ready to take down the pertinent information.

Mrs. Van Winterden slid a piece of paper across the desk. It was a printout of two names, addresses, phone numbers, and biographical notes.

"They are getting married in one hour at City hall. They've given us permission to feature their civil ceremony. I want you to write up their wedding and their reasons for marrying. I need two thousands words by tomorrow, for a piece entitled, 'Weddings without the Fuss.'"

Kit felt bile rise in her throat and the only thing that could have been worse than being fired today was an assignment to write about yet another happy couple. Not to mention that she would be running on espresso all night to pound out two thousand words.

The glare Great White's lenses made it impossible to read the expression in her deep-set eyes. But somehow Kit knew it was one of pure determination. "Fine," Kit said. "I'll get right on it."

Great White checked her watch. "Edgar Lacey should be there by now with a photographer and a simple floral arrangement. There's a limo waiting for you in the parking garage. In it is a box with an additional item for the occasion. Please deliver it to the photographer before the ceremony."

Kit jumped to her feet, trying to ignore the hollow feeling in her stomach. "I'll get right on it." She did not want to watch another couple exchange vows.

Great White seemed to read her mind. "You are, after all, carving out a niche for yourself as our expert on reality-style romance."

The comment might have been well-deserved, but Kit had had enough. Mother's lama would call it the awakening of the sleeping tiger. Edgar would say later it was the moment Kit found her mojo, or more precisely, the moment Kit's mojo found her. "I appreciate the assignment," Kit began.

Great White gave a small nod and turned away.

"Before I go, there's something I need to say."

The founding editor swiveled back again to face Kit.

Kit knew the safe thing would be to leave now, but she could not. She hadn't committed any offense. She had only admitted her feelings, for the first time in her adult life, and imagined that Mark have the same feelings about her. It had been a mistake. But Kit now knew one thing to be true. Life had far more meaning when she allowed herself to take a risk instead of hiding from all its possibilities.

"I apologize for anything I might have done to contribute to this situation." Kit's voice faltered.

Great White's eyes glittered.

"But, the real story behind somebody's wedding is never the one you see when they're making toasts or posing for photographs."

Now it was Mrs. Van Winterden's turn to be surprised, judging by her raised eyebrows.

"The fact is, I've learned a lot on this assignment." Kit paused and drew in a breath. "Namely, you can't turn a marriage into a made-for-TV news story. And a wedding isn't a P.R. opportunity. It's about knowing and telling the truth about what's inside your heart. Planning a great party is one thing. But it shouldn't become so big that it takes on a life of its own, that the people involved don't even know how they feel about what they're doing." Kit's heart was racing so fast she felt dizzy. But she stood straight with her head high and her shoulders back. She had spoken her truth at last.

The room was so quiet Kit could hear the sounds of the outer office. File drawers being slammed, bits of laughter, a copying machine kicking into gear. Normal sounds of people whose futures were not in jeopardy.

Mrs. Van Winterden surveyed Kit thoughtfully. Her tiny mouth opened as if she was about to say something. Then it closed again. Another moment or two passed. Finally, she spoke. "You have an interesting perspective, Ms. McCabe, and frankly one that has not been shared in this magazine. You may, perhaps, explore it further in your assignment. Obviously, a couple who chooses a quiet civil ceremony has a unique perspective."

Kit nodded, amazed that the woman across the table, who could make or break a career with a single email, seemed to be giving careful consideration to the merits of what Kit had said. Maybe, just maybe, Mrs. Van Winterden had not gotten to be the wedding diva by being closed-minded. But that realization was better saved for reflection at another time. Right now, Kit had work to do.

"Right," she said, turning to go, spurred by a new-found energy and purpose. She dashed to the elevator and took it to the underground parking garage. There waited a limo, complete with tinted windows to shield her from the press.

Kit's chariot had arrived.

Chapter Fifteen

Weddings, the Van Winterden Way: To thine own self be true*
*Addendum to second edition, based on articles originally appearing in WHITE WEDDINGS magazine, reprinted with permission of the publisher.

Kit sank into the plush leather seat of the limo and tore into the box she was to deliver to City Hall. White tulle spilled over the sides of the box. Kit groaned and looked away. Tulle only reminded her of the nightmares she'd been having.

She glanced out the window. A light rain had begun to fall, slowing traffic. The limo inched along. At this rate, the bride and groom would leave for their honeymoon before Kit reached City Hall. It would have been faster to take the subway. Still, Kit was grateful to have avoided another run-in with the paparazzi. There was something to be said for limos with tinted windows, she decided.

The FDR was at a standstill. Kit checked her watch. They were running out of time. The driver exited the highway and began to crawl south on side streets.

Kit sighed, and tried to focus on the background notes Mrs. Van Winterden had given her. Another couple in love, who couldn't live without each other. Kit wrinkled her nose. She didn't know how she would manage to sit through a wedding. At least Edgar would be there. She impatiently tapped her fingers on the door and watched raindrops trickle down the car window.

Kit fought the panic that was rising inside her. If she did not do something fast she was going to miss the ceremony. Just south of Canal Street, she decided to run the rest of the way. She instructed the driver to pull over, grabbed the box, and got out.

She trotted south on rain-slicked pavement, ignoring the vendors selling tiny black umbrellas on every corner. There was no way to avoid puddles so she gave up trying. By the time she reached City Hall, heart pounding and soaked to the skin, her navy pumps were ruined. Kit pulled the long veil from its box, now soggy from the rain. She tossed the box into a trash can and raced up the granite steps, her arms full of white tulle.

She followed signs marked "Marriages." She turned down a hallway, the kind that seemed to go on forever. She was late. She ran, her damp shoes skidding on the linoleum floor, until the veil got in her way. Kit's feet got tangled in the tulle and she felt herself fall.

She landed in a sea of white. Hard. She sat for a moment, stunned, as a realization hit her. It was her dream. The long hall, the floors, the tulle. It was all familiar, and eerie except for one thing. Mark Dawson was nowhere to be seen. There were only curious onlookers and a security guard who was reaching out to help her up.

Kit waved off his offer to take her to the first aid station. She dusted herself off and hurried on. She was definitely late now.

She finally reached a door marked "Weddings Today." Inside, the place was packed with excited couples who had decided today was going to be their big day.

Kit elbowed her way to a spot in front. Luckily, she was in the right place.

There was a couple standing in front of a judge. And not just any couple. Her couple. They were dressed in street clothes, and the woman carried an elaborate bouquet of white orchids and long-stemmed white roses wrapped in ivory ribbon. The groom wore a sport coat with a white rose boutonniere courtesy of the *White Weddings* art department, Kit was sure.

Edgar Lacey and the photographer stood nearby, beaming. In fact, everyone was smiling. It was the happiest day of this couple's lives, despite the fact that there were no strolling violins, no ice sculptures, no white wine fountains, and no wedding planner whispering instructions into a tiny mic.

Edgar caught sight of Kit and waved her forward.

Kit placed the white veil atop the bride's head and fluffed it before stepping back into the crowd. The

White Weddings photographer snapped away, his camera whirring as the couple, beaming with joy, exchanged vows in their simple ceremony.

Edgar looked at Kit and winked.

Goosebumps rose on Kit's arms under her damp suit jacket, and she got all choked up—not with the stuffy nose and scratchy throat signaling an allergy attack, but with tears of joy at seeing two people pledge their lives to each other. Here, in a crowded room with bad lighting inside an aging New York City municipal office building in lower Manhattan, with a crowd of strangers looking on, it was real because their love for each other was real.

She did not fight the tears that began to trickle down her face because Kit McCabe was finished fighting her feelings. She had had a brief glimpse of what it felt like to find the perfect man and fall for him, even if it wasn't meant to be. And once a woman had glimpsed true love, she can never feel unloved again.

The realization hit her like a lightning bolt. It was the message in her dream. She had been running toward it in the dream, and just now in real life. Love. Pure love. That, once felt, could never be forgotten. Love changed a person forever. In a good way. Kit sniffed.

A handkerchief was pressed into her hand from behind her.

She accepted it gratefully and dabbed her eyes, noting the familiar scent and feel of the linen. She glanced down and saw a familiar *D*.

Kit whirled around and found herself gathered up in Mark Dawson's arms.

He kissed her passionately.

The moon and stars were in that kiss. It changed Kit's world. She could feel it from her toes all the way up to the top of her head. The room and everyone in it was forgotten as she felt herself swept up in the embrace.

Mark held her even tighter, brushed his lips across her cheek and growled into her ear. "It's about time. I've been trying to track you down since Miami."

Kit looked into his eyes. Twinkling again. Definitely twinkling. She shook her head slowly in disbelief. "I needed to go . . . I thought you and Ruby . . . ," her voice trailed off.

Mark did not loosen his hold, his face just inches from hers. He shook his head, his eyes tender, like a caress. "Kit, I have so much to tell you. Please just give me time to explain."

Kit nodded. She did not trust her voice, and she felt too warm in his embrace to pull away. She breathed in his scent. It was woodsy and good, the way she remembered.

Mark gazed intently into her eyes. "I never felt this way before. Not about any woman. Not until I met you."

She could hardly believe it was real. The fluttering had returned to her stomach, and with it a warm, soothing sensation that was spreading slowly throughout her. She felt like she was floating in a warm bath. She gathered what remained of her strength, however, and pulled her face away from his. She had questions to ask. "Go on."

Mark grinned. "Ever the journalist. It's what I admire most about you."

Kit smiled back. And waited for answers.

"At first I didn't want to believe it," he continued. "But there it was. I had to do something. I didn't want to drag you into it. I didn't want you to risk losing your job. I came up on the next flight after yours and tried all day to track you down." He swallowed, his brown eyes dark and earnest, his voice low and sincere. "More than anything, I didn't want to lose you."

Kit nodded, hardly able to believe her ears.

"When I didn't find you, I went to your office first thing this morning. I met with Mrs. Van Winterden."

Kit's eyes widened in surprise. "You did?"

Mark grinned. "Yep, with her and all the elves."

Kit thought of the P.R. department, the marketing department, and the lawyers who had worked on the contest Mark and Ruby had won. She shook her head in disbelief. "That must have been quite a show."

Mark's gaze softened. "It wasn't so bad. And I got what I wanted. The old girl told me you'd be here."

Now Kit's surprise turned to genuine shock. "Mrs. Van Winterden told you I'd be here?"

Mark nodded, "Turns out she's a softie underneath."

Kit's mind raced back over her meeting with Great White, how she had informed Kit she had planned to fire her. Until something changed her mind. Not something. Someone. She looked at Mark and smiled.

Mark looked at her like he had just won the lottery.

"You mean she doesn't mind the way everything turned out?"

Mark grinned. "I wouldn't worry about it too much. *White Weddings* got all the free publicity they could ask for and then some. Everybody in town will be talking about Ethel Van Winterden's new book. Ruby gets her cable show. And . . . ," His smile was so wide it took up all the space on that chiseled jaw, "I'm the luckiest man in New York. Because I get a chance to work things out with you."

His lips found their way to Kit's and he kissed her the way he had kissed her on the beach. His voice dropped lower. "Correction. I'm the luckiest man in the world." Mark pulled her close and kissed her again.

Kit relaxed against him, enjoying the way his arms felt around her. She closed her eyes until she saw stars again.

When she opened her eyes Mark was gazing down at her, serious now. "Change that again," he growled. "I'm the luckiest man in the universe."

It was an interesting choice of words. Mother's lama would approve.

The room around them broke into applause.

Kit looked over her shoulder. The judge had just declared the civil ceremony couple husband and wife.

Edgar was beaming at Kit from across the room. He flashed her a thumbs up.

She smiled and turned back to Mark. She held still as another wave of pure joy flooded over her. It was a feeling, she suspected, she would become accustomed to because Mark didn't seem willing to loosen his grip any time soon. And that was just fine with Kit.

And it was precisely at this moment that her own karma was revealed to her. Not on a rhododendron trail high in the Himalayas. Not in an ashram near the harmonic convergence in Taos. But right here, in the

New York City Clerk's office on a rainy day in spring. Kit's karma had indeed found her, landing with the force of a ten-ton lorry, only not as messy, as Edgar would say.

Karma was like that.